SOAR

USA TODAY BESTSELLING AUTHOR

Renee Lee Fisher

Credits

Definition of soar –

: to fly aloft or about

: to sail or hover in the air often at a great height

: to rise or increase dramatically (as in position, value, or price)

: to ascend to a higher or more exalted level

: to rise to majestic stature

Definition of sore –

: causing emotional pain or distress

: physically tender; feeling or affected by pain

: attended by difficulties, hardship, or exertion

Suddenly, in a mere blink, we fall in love or we suffer a loss; we just don't know when it will happen. So, hold onto those you love dearly until they slip from your grasp.

Dedication

It's hard to lose someone you love. I still reread her favorite quotes, which she had on her Pinterest page. Below are a few that I have captured to the written page to share.

She whispers, "I'm afraid of falling."
He offers a sincere smile. "I'll always catch you."

A blessing and curse to feel everything so deeply.

Should I travel to the left, where nothing seems right, or to the right where nothing is left?

The most beautiful part is I wasn't ever looking when you came along.

The way they leave you tells me everything.

Be alone or step forward.

The best sound is my name heard from your lips.

And in the end, all I learned was how strong to be alone.

Life is a balance of holding on and letting go, especially

where the heart is concerned.

My heart is thousands of years old; I am not like other people.

Two souls that didn't find one another by accident.

I told the stars above about you.

You were my plot twist.

We are all made of stardust to shimmer and shine.

It's the *heart* that really matters in the end. – Rob Thomas

Prelude

I**T WAS AN** average weekend day. Free time when most of us who continued to be friends post high school gathered to hang out. It could be for a simple lunch or a small party, but this day it was to head to the lake. The water was inviting with the warmth of the day. When most people say they need R&R—rest and relaxation—these friends meant a day at Ridge Rock Lake when they said it. The setting was beautiful, with plenty to do from swimming and hiking, to biking and canoeing. This summer's day, most were seen cooling off in the lake's offering of refreshing water.

Rayleigh Mitchell stood tall about five feet nine inches with her denim shorts and pink floral tank top. She hadn't worn her bathing suit as she didn't have plans of swimming this particular day. Jeweled flip flops—her favorite go-to shoes—carried her along the lakeside for a lovely view. Her toes felt the wetness and it was a tease as she would loved to have dove in for a swim. Her long, blonde hair fell to both sides of her shoulders, getting lighter in the summertime.

Her amber-colored eyes were hidden by her sunglasses, but her dusty rose lip gloss shimmered with the rays of the sun.

"Rayleigh, aren't you staying?" a voice hollered out from Monroe, her best friend.

"Actually, I've enjoyed the day with you all but I have to get to work. Perhaps next time I can stay longer." Rayleigh glanced at everyone. She knew they would deem her a party pooper, but she had to get to the hospital—she was doing her clinicals after putting off nursing school until recently. At least now she was pursuing her career. Some of the others still were a bit career misdirected and living life on the edge. Rayleigh had long since lightened up her drinking days and staying out 'til all hours. Just being amongst everyone here today was tiresome.

"Come on, Rayleigh … please honor us with your presence the rest of today. It's not the same without you," Monroe attempted a second request.

Her bestie's plea was fruitless. Rayleigh knew she had to think smart. Her obligations for student loans and schooling caused her to decline.

"Bye, and everyone have fun." Rayleigh didn't turn back; she got to her car and drove off to her apartment to change and head into a night of work at Northview Hospital located in the suburbs of Philadelphia, Pennsylvania.

GAZING OUT THE sliding glass door to the balcony of her apartment the following morning, she saw that everything was cast in grey. Rayleigh was glad to have had the chance to have fun in the sun yesterday. Her eyes still carried the tears from the late-night patient who came into the hospital, dead on arrival. Despite attempting to forget what happened, pretend it wasn't true, it kept repeating in her mind this morning, and would for a long time to come.

Leaving everyone yesterday was hard because Rayleigh was having a great time. She was told they continued to drink and challenge one another to jumping off the old bridge that remained once the new, wider lane one was installed. The old, rusty bridge hung over the far corner of the lake. It wasn't that it was too high up, it was that sometimes the water line in that area was too low. If one wasn't thinking properly, they could be making a very fatal jump.

Which is exactly what happened. Rayleigh was told the one in the entire group closest to her was challenged by the others, and opted to be the first to jump and set the standards for the rest. Being a diver on the swim team in high school this seemed a cake walk. She jumped and did an amazing flip in the air followed by cheers. She broke through the water surface with precision … only never surfaced until it was too late. The lake was low and she plunged too hard, too fast. Without warning her life ended tragically.

Such a loss of life, too early on. A painful absence for her family and friends, and also Rayleigh who wasn't there when it happened but got a first, up-close visual when the paramedics brought her body into emergency.

"I should never have left them. I should have stayed," Rayleigh said to herself, knowing she was on the verge of crying hard. Not that her staying would have changed anything. There was a void within her, that was like losing a part of herself. Her best friend was gone. Forever.

There is a moment after someone who you held in your heart passes that you ... break. Our body folds into the anguish of such a loss. Rayleigh delicately took hold of her hand to offer the deceased a comforting final touch. For Rayleigh, she tried to remain stoic and professional at the hospital where she worked, but she couldn't hold back the tears nor did she have the strength in her legs to stand tall. She was barely able to walk with weakened limbs to the next empty emergency bed area. There her body fell on top of the gurney and she let herself succumb to the heart-wrenching news of the death of the person they just brought into the emergency area.

Rubbing her wet eyes hard, Rayleigh tried to wipe away the sight of someone she loved who didn't make it. Didn't breathe another breath. Just remained motionless. Monroe—who earlier in the day pleaded with Rayleigh to stay—laid lifeless and was now gone…forever. Monroe was not her real name; she dubbed herself that nickname early on in high school as she had such admiration for anything Marilyn Monroe. Rayleigh always called her by her real name when just the two of them were together.

There would never be another Monroe in the circle of friends as she was a legend in herself. She was fearless, outspoken, and a definite risk taker. A petite girl with a lot of power from within. If one were to say, "No," to her, she would counter with, "No way!" and keep moving forward. She never let things get in her way, she would simply walk over them. Rayleigh was so opposite—she had many fears, was a romantic, and lived life peacefully. Rayleigh always thought before she reacted, and she knew that although she left all her friends at the lake that Monroe was fearless and would never have foreseen the harm or danger lying beneath the water when she dove in. Rayleigh could envision Monroe taking the challenge to dive in first. Monroe would now float above forever and challenge the afterlife with her being. Such a young loss and so tragic.

Helplessness … Rayleigh felt absolute helplessness. No matter if a family member, close friend, or chance meeting with a person, if they at all touched your heart you would feel the pain of their departure from this world.

Rayleigh clenched her chest as she curled into herself on the metal gurney, only to feel the excruciating pain within her own heart. An emptiness that she would never fill again with this person in her life. Although she'd seen daily wounds and sickness, and even death, Rayleigh was not prepared for this. This one would linger with her forever. Knowing she was lying several feet from the girl who came in dead on arrival, Rayleigh tried desperately to hold back her tears and muffle her whimpering. She turned her head deep into the pillow provided for the patients and pulled the white sheet and thin beige blanket up over her, seeking comfort.

There's no manual in the medical training that told you

how to stifle your emotions at this moment. All the help and serving an ailing person will seem useless when you find you are unable to save another. No one could have predicted what happened at the lake. It was a tragic loss. When Rayleigh left all her friends to go to work, she didn't look back because this one lying dead just feet away from her would have convinced her to stay and blow off work for the day. They had a closeness amongst the group of friends and had shared a lot of fun together, only they didn't agree with whom each other dated nor who each had chosen for a best friend.

Sadly, another bright light of a person had gone out. Rayleigh heard a male voice—the attending doctor—on the other side of the curtain giving the final directions. She tightened her eyelids and fists to curb the ache that surged within her.

An earlier day of the sun shining and warmth embracing everyone that gathered for a good time at the lake was splashed over with death and immense sorrow.

Chapter One

GRIEF CAN GRASP onto you and place you in permanent despair, or you can rise and go forth day to day the best you can, never forgetting a lost loved one but keeping their memories close. Rayleigh lost her best friend, her soul mate, a part of her heart a few months ago and she has chosen to try to put herself back into the world in life and love with what remains in her heart. Rayleigh kept a distance from her circle of friends as being with them wasn't comforting but a constant reminder of the loss of one of them. She kept more to herself since the unforeseen accident occurred.

No one really wants to be alone; emptiness now filled the rooms where long talks and laughter once was shared. Missing her previous best friend that she roomed with, Rayleigh thought of again sharing her large, two-bedroom apartment. As quickly as she placed the advertisement for a roommate, she happily found one and removed her search from the newspaper. It had only been posted for a weekend, and she knew right away the person was fit to live with her, as they clicked immediately. Alissa was her name. New roommate spot was successfully filled, and so was her apartment with another to keep her company. Rayleigh described Alissa as more forward, opinionated where she lacked. Alissa stood about five feet three, and dressed simply in torn jeans. Her hair was shoulder-length, straight, and a sandy brown color. Her eyes of a soft chestnut brown shone warmth to Rayleigh.

In the days that followed she was glad she pulled the ad quickly to interview potential roommates. She was very satisfied with her current living situation.

Now that she seemed to have a perfect roommate, she decided to work on her love life, which was far from that. She was determined to put herself out there to meet someone, perhaps then her heart would be full once more. Most days Rayleigh spent her free time on social media sites because that was the ideal way nowadays to find a potential mate. To her it appeared clinical, but she continued to go onto the various sites, hopeful she would click with a match.

It happened all too quickly, though, that she met Roden. He was from California, and despite the time change between them—between the east to the west—everything else was perfect … or was it? Alissa immediately thought different, and she was far from shy in voicing her opinions on this man.

Rayleigh could hear Alissa telling her, "It's too perfect. How can he like *everything* you do? I'm calling it a set up, or fake, so please be careful. Just saying I think it is all fishy.

Not simply you catching him but vice versa."

Rayleigh listened to her warning but that didn't distract her at all, as she typed to him a very suggestive message.

Roden, let's do it! I mean meet and go away together. I'm thinking sandy beach, sunsets to die for, and Mai Tai drinks ... how about Hawaii?

You read my mind, Rayleigh. Sounds perfect! And of course, a Lei ... or was that a typo on my part as I'm being forward and thinking more that I meant lay? LOL

Roden, I'm right there with you. I like your forwardness. I'll find us an all-inclusive vacation spot. We can fly separately from our states and meet there. I know we will have a blast. What a first meeting this will be.

Rayleigh, the sooner you book this the faster we can meet. Let me know the details and I will book my flight from here. I can only hope to arrive before you so I can capture you in my arms the moment our eyes meet for real.

Rayleigh fidgeted in her seat. She was definitely overdo for sex and her attraction to Roden appeared so real already. He was gorgeous. All of his profile photos screamed *hot!* Rayleigh was fit herself and could hold her own in a bikini so she wasn't sweating their initial meeting. As Roden continued to message her, she was on another site planning a getaway to a couples only resort in Hawaii. She had never been to that area before, but it was certainly on her bucket list of destinations to share with someone she was romantically interested in.

Rayleigh, I already imagine holding you next to me ... I can't wait to take our relationship to the next level. To touch you, to kiss you, and to finally be inside of you.

Her vagina lit up on fire with his last line. **Mmmm, sounds so inviting. Soon, Roden, and I can't wait to meet you and everything else.**

Her concentration was instantly broken from having sex with Roden to hearing Alissa interrupt her.

"Seriously, Rayleigh, are you planning a trip? You don't even know him."

"I know him better than you think, and I know what I want," Rayleigh exclaimed.

"I don't think you do." Alissa shook her head, her sandy brown hair brushing the tops of her shoulders. "Watch out is all I can tell you."

"I don't need a mother looking after me. I am an adult."

Alissa's brow furrowed. "You need me. Trust me, you do." With that, Alissa took her coffee mug and left the room.

Rayleigh put her head to her computer, wanting to get back into the mood that Roden was setting up for her. Needing a release from her sexual frustration. Unfortunately, Alissa ruined the moment for her.

Soon, though, she would be off on a vacation and completely alone with Roden and no distractions.

Back onto the planning of a trip, she thought. Rayleigh located a last-minute deal for two weeks ahead. Her fingers found her credit card, and she booked the ocean view suite. Next, she purchased her airfare and sent her details to Roden.

Forty minutes later, she received his text.

**Rayleigh, this is great. I booked my flight and as luck has it, I arrive 2 hours prior to you. I will be at the resort waiting for you. Just thinking of this has me hard already. Let me pay

for the resort stay. If not now, I will take care of that once I arrive. After all, a gentleman should handle all these details of whisking you away. You have done too much already.

Rayleigh smiled, planning to carry the elated feeling for the next fourteen days until she finally was in the arms of Roden. Not listening to anything Alissa suggested, she already made her way to get her suitcase and start packing.

RAYLEIGH HAD THE opportunity to finally take a vacation. Working at the hospital many hours and taking on additional shifts to fill her void of no life, she accumulated some much-needed time off.

She was set to venture out later to buy toiletries to pack and some sexy lingerie as most days she slept in oversized men's lounging pants and a tee shirt. Nothing like that speaks sexy. Also, she wanted to stop at the local florist to get an arrangement of fresh flowers for her apartment.

"Another order of the same florals, Miss Rayleigh?" asked the teenager behind the counter at Sunny Side Flowers.

She nodded. Her hands took hold of the deep red roses and the burgundy calla lilies, and when the fragrance hit her nose, her eyes moistened from a moment of sadness. "Thank you, they are beautiful as always."

ONCE BACK HOME after returning from running all around, Rayleigh began putting a few of the bags on the counter. As she reached for a vase from the kitchen shelf, she noticed her roommate's presence. A smile formed on her lips as Rayleigh arranged the florals and topped the vase off with fresh water. Now their beauty would thrive for days. The flowers brightened up her white wood kitchen table surrounded by white chairs. Rayleigh had a modern décor within her apartment; a gray sectional set in her living room with a slate coffee table. She had added pillows but they were cream, not a real pop of color. Black and white artwork hung on the walls—some photos of friends and some of her family. Setting the vase on the table, she glanced at the far wall of a photograph of someone she loved and lost. A moment of sadness overcame her in her own surroundings. After a few seconds, she took her eyes off the wall and onto the colorful flowers where a smile appeared on her face. She smiled warmly when her roommate said the exact same words that the floral sales person had earlier.

Alissa commented, "The flowers are beautiful as always. I never get tired of seeing them here in the apartment."

It wasn't just the lovely flowers, nor the scent that carried through the apartment, Rayleigh sensed Alissa wanting her attention. As she inhaled the aroma from the flowers, Rayleigh heard Alissa freely offering her opinions yet again.

"Listen, I know you are older than me, but not by much … I'm just telling you what I think. Rayleigh, that man, Roden, is not for you."

"Alissa, I hear you, I've heard your advice, but could you do me a favor and perhaps go fly a kite today in the park that you so love? It's beautiful outside, and you are getting much better in your kite flying capabilities. Please leave me here to continue floating in my own happiness of falling further for Roden."

"I loved flying kites … so glad you remembered, but not today as I'm having much more enjoyment hovering over you," Alissa countered playfully.

"Ugh, I can't win. Somedays I love you as my roommate and other days I wish I left the advertisement run longer to gain other prospective applicants." Rayleigh laughed. She knew Alissa had well learned her humor and that she was only kidding.

WITH THE TRIP coming up quickly, Rayleigh had to get a move on packing. As she was fighting in her living room closet to reach and remove her navy suitcase, she tossed out a few old coats to the floor, which she felt she could donate and make more room instead of losing the battle between all the full hangers every time.

She laughed to herself when she turned back toward the

living room area proudly with her suitcase in hand. What made her smile was not the battle of winning the suitcase handle from deep in the closet, but seeing Alissa wearing Rayleigh's high school cheerleading jacket. It reminded her of long ago when her younger sister wore it and it was too big on her. Rayleigh recalled her sister looking up to her accomplishment of being a cheerleader. Her sister didn't much like school, only the friends she made along the way. Most of her sister's education was life lessons taught after those earlier years.

"I need to give some of these old coats away, there are too many piled in that front closet," Rayleigh commented, and still smiled observing Alissa modeling the high school jacket. Alissa twirled, displaying the bold, gold letters and the team mascot of a ram adorning the old piece of clothing.

In an attempt for diversion of Alissa making any sarcastic comments about her holding the suitcase, Rayleigh set it down and went to turn on the television. It was game day. She knew all too well that her roommate was a diehard lover of the Dallas team and said their cheerleaders were the best. If anything could turn her head and gain her attention it would be the game on the screen.

Success! It worked. Alissa moved toward the television as the teams were forming within their huddle. When Rayleigh glanced at the score in the corner of the screen, she saw that Alissa's favorite team was winning and there she sat in front watching the game, still wearing the jacket. This was a brilliant idea as it enabled Rayleigh to slip away for another twelve minutes—at least that was left in the quarter of the game—to throw things into her suitcase with peace and quiet and no advice from Alissa on her upcoming travel plans. Plus, she wanted to pack her smallest bikini and sexiest lingerie and keep that a secret to herself.

Alissa was a great roommate, and when Rayleigh thought of not having her company, she knew it would leave her lonely. Plus, you can't simply remove someone from your life just because you have differences of opinions and more. It was nice having Alissa there to challenge her daily with most of Rayleigh's decisions, especially when a male was the topic.

Chapter Two

"YOU'RE BEING STUPID," a familiar voice shouted into Rayleigh's ears as she parked at the airport. Normally, one would be driving erratically from the sudden voice she heard, but she was used to it. She could just roll her eyes and ignore it to the best of her abilities.

There are many reasons for that. One of it was that the person she kept hearing advice or opinions from was Alissa. Even now, well out of her range to engage in conversation with Alissa, she still was thinking of what she would be telling her to do or not to do. Rayleigh chuckled to herself, glad she was venturing solo on this trip and not a girls' vacation.

"Look. It's my only shot of love. I have to take the chance," Rayleigh returned heatedly in a loud voice to herself. It was tough to have someone question her every step of the way. Alissa had certainly tried. From the first moment she had met Roden online, she had been vocal about her dislike of him. This wasn't even counting the many ways she had tried to stop her from leaving for the airport. Rayleigh swore she packed everything necessary into her suitcase, but when she went to double check, things were missing. She only hoped she recaptured all the items she needed before she left. At least her sexy lingerie … although she was hoping to not have that on too long with Roden.

All in all, Alissa's attempts to keep her grounded and miss the trip weren't successful.

Rayleigh managed to get past her obstructions, and even came here three hours early, all pumped up and excited for the trip alone with Roden. This was their first time meeting each other and it would be at the romantic island of Hawaii. She couldn't wait.

The only downside was that Alissa would be coming with them per se. Rayleigh still thought about her room-mate's words.

"Why is this your only shot at romance? There's plenty of other men out there," Alissa cried out, waving her arm and gesturing to the world outside of the car before Rayleigh had left to the airport. Rayleigh couldn't believe she even said that. For now, Rayleigh needed to tamp down those thoughts—especially where Alissa was concerned—and focus on something much more important … *Roden.*

The reality was, no matter how much she'd tried, all of Rayleigh's dates hadn't worked out. And she had tried so hard. She changed her hairstyle once, her makeup, but nothing worked. Resting her head on the leather head rest, she again heard Alissa reciting more ways to meet men in the real world, not on the computer.

She just wouldn't understand.

As roomies, they hit it off great. They were very close in age. Their looks differed, their hair color was opposite light versus dark, their eyes, too. Rayleigh had the height advantage at 5'9" over Alissa's shorter frame. They could still choose to share clothes, only some things would be much shorter on Rayleigh as there was about a six-inch height difference, or vice versa some clothes may be too long on Alissa. Their only main difference was they had very dissimilar taste in men. Rayleigh never lectured Alissa on whom to date or to not date, but always received Alissa's out spoken opinions even when not asked for them.

Rayleigh was the more light-hearted of the two. She liked to laugh and surround herself with people. If given a choice, she would call herself an extrovert, sometimes taken advantage of. Alissa would remind her of such.

Alissa was the quieter of the two until she got to know you better. She didn't really like to be around new people. The ones she called friends were those she really liked; people she would put her life on the line for. She was the type of person who either really loved or hated someone. There was no middle ground.

After conversing earlier this week with her roommate—which most women do often late into the night—Rayleigh confessed for some reason, she had always chosen the wrong guy. When she entered a relationship, she gave her all into it. She tried to spend as much time as possible with him, getting to know his likes and dislikes, meeting his friends and family. All of that usually went to dust quickly when he broke her heart in the worst way possible. The most awful one that came to mind was the guy who used her to get close to Alissa. Even though Alissa didn't do anything except to rebuff him harshly, it still hurt.

That's why she was so excited to meet Roden, having come across his profile on a dating site she hadn't heard of before, because it was not one of the one's advertised. She liked what she saw. Rayleigh had been instantly intrigued and told herself it wasn't a waste of her time to pursue this site. Her heart raced at the sight of his photo. Of course, what caught her eyes first was his looks. He was very sexy ... hot. Sun-kissed brown hair, bright blue eyes, accompanied by his perfect white smile. After first glance, she actually read his profile and her interest deepened. He was an outgoing guy with interests ranging from skiing, kick boxing, hiking, and adventurous traveling. These were things she had always wanted to try out but never had the chance. Until now, that is, as she was about to venture on her first time traveling with a romantic man.

Returning back to her thoughts of when they met online, she recalled that he had sent the first message and she found him to be fun, a very witty conversationalist. They messaged each other to the late hours of most nights. Sometimes, she went to work tired after a night with him ... conversing that is.

The only downside was that he lived on the other side of the coast. She was disappointed when she discovered he was living in California. They agreed they would message more online to get to know one another. They exchanged many photos, many personal thoughts … and several deeper sexual conversations. She couldn't explain it but she hadn't felt like this with anyone else before.

Chapter Three

ONE DAY, THE topic to meet up came up. He had mentioned going to Hawaii for some surfing and it sounded so fun. Since she had some vacation time, she suggested with her heart in her throat that they meet up.

There was a couple of heart-stopping seconds before he messaged yes. She had been so happy that she jumped around her room. Alissa was less than happy as she had never liked the guy. And she tried to dissuade Rayleigh from going but she wasn't listening.

This would be the love of her life. She was going to meet him and fall irrevocably in love. They were going to get married and live together in harmony. She had even pictured the kids they were going to have. They were going to be so attractive.

RAYLEIGH WAS GETTING ahead of her future already with wonderful thoughts, but for now it was time to take off for her flight to love, bliss, and hopes of hot sex. She had to get moving and stop her daydreaming. Despite it being two hours until the flight, she got out of the car. There was nothing else to do in the car. Grabbing her luggage, she made her way to the terminal, the butterflies in her stomach fluttering so much that it felt like there was a hurricane.

Even the waiting time didn't calm them down. She almost had a panic attack. Her heart was pounding extremely hard and it was difficult to breath. Then it was time to fly.

By the time she landed, she managed to get her composure back. At the baggage collection area, she was looking around, feeling confused. This was her first trip to Hawaii and there were so many people. Almost drowning in the cacophony, she nearly screamed when someone tapped her shoulder. Turning around hesitantly, her head went light-headed when the perfection greeted her.

"Hi. Are you Rayleigh?" a man who looked exactly like Roden asked.

Her heart nearly burst out of her chest. He looked much better in person. The photos and messages didn't capture his energy.

"Y-Yes. Roden?"

"I wanted to meet you at the airport since my flight from California was shorter than yours," he responded with a sexy smile.

That romantic gesture almost did her in. *Why does that make him look hotter?*

Then, he took her bag from her hand and nodded his head to where she figured the exit was. "Come on. Let's get to our resort where we will surely get to know one another much better."

Like the game pin the tail on the donkey, she blindly followed him.

Although he was the one who spoke the most, they had a nice talk in the cab. She was too overwhelmed by this unexpected kindness and the impact he had on her. If he was this eager, did that mean he was as excited to meet her as she was him?

Not wanting to get her hopes up, she tried her best to keep her cool. But he made it incredibly hard. He helped them check in to their beach view suite. Then, being the gentleman that he was, she noted he refrained from coming onto her immediately once they were alone in the vast suite, which had a king-sized bed front and center with sheer curtains surrounding it blowing in the ocean breeze.

"Rayleigh, as inviting as this suite is, and as amazing as it is to have you here with me, we can wait to be together until you feel totally comfortable."

Her lips parted to reply, but all she could think about was her vagina, which was about to explode because of how desperately she needed sex.

This was like a dream come true. He was everything she could wish for. He was brilliant, considerate, and kind. Since she'd been nervous, he controlled their conversation during the drive so it had barely faltered. It was like chatting online but she could actually see his face, hear his voice, and touch him for real.

Just thinking about him made her heart beat faster and her breath hitch. Rayleigh thought, *is this really going to happen this soon? Are Roden and I going to sleep together?* On one hand, this was the first time they were meeting—it was a bit presumptuous to think that. However, they had known each other for a while, at least with all their cyber conversing.

Not that she had asked him about sex outright. That screamed desperate like nothing else. The topic had surfaced one night, and soon they further discussed being eager in their exchanged words to meet and come together and share their romance and a bed.

Catching him eyeing her in the center of the suite, her heart jumped to her throat when she received his sexy stare. Every time she glanced his way, she was struck by his sheer beauty. He looked like he should be a model. *An underwear model*, came to Rayleigh's mind. Clad in a crisp, white shirt and faded jeans, he was good enough to eat. She believed she wasn't alone in thinking that. Rayleigh was ready, so ready to take the plunge, and without regret her decision was to throw herself at him.

His sexy eyes bore heat through her. This had never happened before, so she was going to bask in it for however long. Most importantly, though, her eyes also duly noted that huge, empty king bed. *This is how the night's going to end*, she perceived.

Taking hold of her hand, Roden led her …

THEIR TRAVELS TO Hawaii were many hours for both of them, and before the night would unfold, they both needed nourishment in the means of food. Rayleigh followed his pull as they went to the restaurant for a meal. She temporarily forgot all about sex during dinner. They had such a great time that everything went out of her head. After dinner, they took a walk down the beach and she found herself falling even deeper in love with him. It was only when they were waiting for the elevator that she remembered her plan—perhaps to try to seduce him innocently and not needy. She tried giving her best shot, though.

"H-How is our evening going to end? This is our first real date." She blinked her eyelashes up at him.

He was silent as he took in her adorable look of uncertainty. When he finally gave her a response, it would assure her an answer of the night's outcome.

"Rayleigh, let me show you the perfect ending."

With those words, a fire was lit under them. It felt like a race to their room after that. She even struggled to open the door. What had been so easy earlier felt like a puzzle in the heat of the moment. The simple key card fumbled in her fingers too many times until finally the green light appeared. *Go!* It was her time for sex once they were through the doorway.

No words were spoken when they stepped in. She threw

herself at him, jumping up and covering his mouth with her lips. Roden was ready for her, catching her without even stumbling. Her heart, which had already been racing by then, was about to explode.

Pushing down on his chest and then tunneling her hands under his shirt, she couldn't believe how good his skin felt to her hands.

Roden responded as his fingers explored her, too. It was as if he could read her body like an open book, each touch like turning a page and increasing the anticipation of him soon deep inside of her. The way he touched her made her feel amazing.

HONK

Rayleigh heard a loud horn. Her first thought was, *Hell no, this better not be a fire alarm in the hotel.* Her body was completely on fire and she was waiting patiently for Roden to put that out.

Again, it sounded, but twice this time.

HONK … HONK

Why was there a car horn sounding? Or was it a hotel alarm increasing to get all the guests' attention? They were on the eighth floor, removing their clothing and about to lower themselves to the fluffy, white bedding. It was probably a hallucination. Shaking her head, she returned to Roden. Being interrupted with the noise, it was tough to immerse herself in the moment again. The honking sound continued, relentlessly.

Looking around, frustrated and pissed off, Rayleigh was about to call the front desk when everything disappeared. Suddenly, she found herself still seated in her car. Her eyes felt gritty and her neck hurt. Blinking rapidly and rubbing her eyes, she realized she was at the airport, her luggage remained in the backseat.

Cars were still honking, trying to keep the airport traffic moving. Often people lingered in spaces that tied up the flow of the traffic—people saying lengthy good-byes, or taking their time in grabbing their belongings, can cause many cars to be at a standstill.

Rayleigh must have fallen asleep. Which made sense since it was hard to sleep last night. She had been stuck between excitement and nervousness. Alissa hadn't helped with the many ways she tried to dissuade Rayleigh from taking the vacation with a man she didn't even know.

Stretching her arms, she looked at the time. There was still time. Her flight was supposed to be at two and it was now six in the evening—

Wait. Her eyes widened. She had to rub them again. That couldn't be the time. She had come here three hours early to make sure she didn't miss her flight. Did she really just miss her flight?

"You finally woke up," she could almost hear Alissa telling her. "Leave, he's not the man for you."

Rayleigh got out of her car and looked around. Sure enough, the sky was turning the bright beautiful orange that characterized day was becoming night. A scream was working its way to her mouth to holler out in the parking lot, but then she thought about Roden.

Oh no. Her hand came up to cover her mouth. If he was anything like her dream, he could be waiting for her at the airport right now in Hawaii or at the resort. What was he going to do if she didn't come? He was so nice and wonderful, the last thing she wanted to do was keep him waiting or start their first meeting delayed. She couldn't have that. She needed to get on the next flight out. But before that, she had to call him, and try to explain how she fell deep asleep and missed her original flight. Surely, he would understand, and still wait for her to come and welcome her in his arms when she arrived delayed just as he had when she dreamt of him.

Dialing his number, she was surprised to hear that the call wouldn't connect. Trying again, she received the same message. That should have rung some bells, but she was too caught up in the thought that he might still be waiting for her.

Her next try was to check his social media page and message him there, but she couldn't find his profile or page anymore. At this time, it finally occurred to her that maybe everything wasn't what it seemed. But he wouldn't do that. He was nice and funny. Not sly and cunning. Definitely not one to catfish another … or so she thought.

As more time passed and her attempts failed one after the other, she had to accept the facts. Her sight blurred and tears began falling. He had indeed catfished her. She didn't know whether Roden even existed or whether he was actually a "he". He could definitely be a she for all she knew.

The one thing she was certain about was that she had been cheated. Out of her money and time. The worst thing was that she had paid for everything. Every. Single. Thing. From her flight to the resort suite … a freaking amazing, expensive suite. It was on her credit card. Someone was using this vacation, only not her and Roden—which may not have been his real name at all. She was scammed.

She felt so dumb. The signs were all there. She booked the trip for them herself and sent Roden the itinerary. He said he would arrive at the resort and give them his credit card to cover their stay. That should have been the first bell, her paying for it initially. She had been so caught up on the idea that he was the one for her that nothing else registered.

Once again, she had thrown out her brain and common sense at the first whiff of love. This wasn't even the first time. However, this was going to be the last. It was getting tiring. At this age, she should have learned her lesson. This was the impetus to do so.

Wiping her face, she took a deep breath. Fortunately, Alissa didn't say anything in her head. Rayleigh was certain that Alissa would have given her an earful very soon.

In silence and tears, she drove out of the lot, to return home hopelessly not in love again.

Chapter Four

A FEW MONTHS *had passed, and Roden was a vague, bad memory.*

Rayleigh was feeling better but her heart was slowly petrifying where men were concerned. It wasn't long before it became a hard piece of stone. Nothing moved it anymore. Her usual love for romance and finding a relationship was gone. She couldn't even watch any romance movies over and over as she once did as they made her life look pathetic. Everything made her fill with apathy and disgust. She actually took to wearing a ring of Alissa's that she long admired and it seemed to keep most males at a distance as she chose to were it on her left hand. It silently spoke she may be engaged and she was never questioned about it. She liked it so much that even if a day came that she met a perfect man for her future, she decided whatever ring they proposed with would have to complement the one already securing that finger. Then again, Rayleigh didn't foresee that ever happening to her. Roommates are known for sharing clothes, food, dreams, and lengthy talks. This ring was one keepsake that Rayleigh was going to hold onto, especially because Alissa told her a while back that she wanted her to have it. Better that Rayleigh wear it than the ring stay hidden inside of Alissa's jewelry chest.

Despite being saddened in the dating world, she was still her usual bright self at work at the hospital and outside of there in public. Even though she was turning into a loveless woman, she didn't feel the need to subject others to it. No one at work knew the devastation she had felt losing love, yet again. If asked she would just say that it didn't work out. Rayleigh chalked it up as he wasn't the *one*.

That was a double-edged sword to her being pretty and single. Friends from the past tried to meet up with her and offer to fix her up on blind dates but she continued to not connect with them. Pain in her heart held her back from allowing herself to submerge herself in fun times with them, let alone let them attempt to find her a man to fill her heart.

As flattered as she felt that still after months passed that they wanted to reach out to her, Rayleigh just wasn't ready for a day at the lake with that crew, she wasn't certain she could ever return there again. She still needed time, more time to process a heartfelt loss. There is not a timeframe for how long to mourn and grieve. Thinking of her few past guys she dated that also left her an emptiness in her heart. She was just tiring of the hurt and not feeling the happiness one should. For now, she needed time for herself—focus on her work, enjoying shared moments with her roommate, Alissa, and live day by day.

For once, Alissa didn't say anything much because no man was in Rayleigh's life at the moment. This was different, having Alissa quieted. Rayleigh enjoyed it, but a part of her was waiting for the other shoe to drop.

As Rayleigh predicted, that reprieve soon ended when she met Matt.

RAYLEIGH MET MATT at a local coffee shop. Perfect Cup was the sign displayed over the entrance door. It claimed to serve just that. It was very simple and innocent their initial connection. She had been there waiting for a coworker to share coffee with after a long hospital shift, when *he* took the empty seat across from her. Seeing as the place was full, she let him share a table. It helped that he was easy on the eyes.

With his dark hair cut short and his warm, chocolate brown eyes, she felt comfortable around him. He looked like he could be on the front page of a business magazine, dressed well and put together. He wore a white shirt and navy pants, and a perfectly chosen yellow tie with some bold blue streaks completed his look. She kept peering at him to make sure she wasn't sharing a table with a celebrity or congressman or such. His perfect smile wasn't practiced; it was offered to her sweetly.

Apart from that, they didn't converse with each other. As her luck would have it, she knocked over her coffee mug.

However, she wondered how that had happened. It had been a heavy ceramic mug. Surely her light, accidental tap wouldn't have toppled it over. There must have been a divine intervention tipping it.

The fact of the matter was that it had. Unfortunately, when it was knocked over, the hot drink flowed in his direction and he scrambled to his feet. She hurried to his side, hoping and praying that none of that got on him, nor burned him.

She wasn't so fortunate. There was a big splash of dark brown on his otherwise pristine white shirt. Grabbing some napkins, she tried to wipe it away, knowing her attempt was futile. The sheer amount of coffee was too much for the tiny paper napkin to conquer. The coffee shop employee was already rushing over to wipe the table and mop the floor. All Rayleigh could do was look over at her newly made mess in helplessness. Through it all, he didn't say anything. He was very calm.

Bracing herself for anger and recrimination, she was surprised when she heard him chuckle. Looking up at him, she could see the laughter coming from him but her disbelief was strong. Was she really seeing this? Was he really laughing, or playing it off to embarrass her even more?

It didn't appear to be a funny situation. A large cup of coffee just spilled all over him. Half of his shirt and pants were covered with it. The only saving grace was the fact that her coffee had been sitting for a while, so it was, if anything, just warm. Otherwise, he would be suffering from some kind of burn.

Suddenly, he laughed harder.

"I-I'm sorry," he wheezed, attempting to tamp down his amusement.

She didn't know what to do. She wanted to apologize, yet it felt weird doing so when he was barely containing himself, but she didn't just want to leave. It was apparent that everyone in the coffee shop was watching them. No way could she flee her own self-made disaster scene.

"I'm the one who should say sorry. It's my coffee that's all over you," she said, hovering over him awkwardly. She still wanted to pat at his shirt. Rayleigh had already offered that during the heat of the moment. Now that some time had passed, it felt inappropriate to do so. She could just hand him some napkins to wipe himself with. "Look. Is there anything I can do to make up for this? I feel so bad."

"No worries. It's not like you did that deliberately. I am one who finds humor in most happenings. Life is too short for upset," he said. "It's only coffee, and I know how to wash my own clothes. The reason I laughed so much is every time I wear a new, white shirt, I wind up getting something spilled on it. However, it's usually by my own doing. Felt good this time that I wasn't at fault for the mishap."

"No, it was all my doing. I have to do something. How about I buy you another cup of coffee … Ah, maybe not the best idea," she said, quickly retracting her offer when she looked down at his shirt. But that was the only thing she could think of. What else could she do?

"How about you and I do dinner?" He flashed a smile toward her.

"What?"

"I like a beautiful woman such as yourself wanting to make this coffee scenario better, and besides, we both have to eat at some point, so that is what you can do. What do you think?"

"I don't know." She really didn't know what to think. Was this guy asking her out for a date? It certainly sounded like a date, right? Or was she thinking too much? Maybe she should try blowing him off. "It's just coffee ... maybe we could do coffee again some time."

"To be honest, we already tried the coffee date and it didn't work so well. Therefore, I think dinner would be better. After all, this is as much for you as it is for me." He sounded so serious and convincing. "My name is Matt Branson and I'm very glad we met today." He studied her with earnest eyes.

"Matt ..." Rayleigh paused as she almost agreed. It was as if he read her mind; he had touched a sadness she was holding in. "Look, to be honest, it'd be nice to dine out with someone. I've been eating in for months, and I have to wonder what it feels like to be with others again." She gave in. He didn't have to even try hard or be relentless. She couldn't help the smile. "But just so we're clear, it's only for a simple dinner. Nothing more. Let's also be clear, no coffee is to be served at our restaurant table. Or perhaps we could request to have our drinks served in child sippy cups." Rayleigh laughed aloud.

"Great. Agreed, no coffee or hot drinks unless with lids tightly affixed." He chuckled again.

Rayleigh noticed that his smile was warm. They exchanged numbers, and she agreed to set up a time and place.

Then she decided to leave the coffee shop before Matt did, when she received a text that her coworker was not going to meet up with her after all. Rayleigh turned to leave. "Rayleigh, my name is Rayleigh." Directing those words toward Matt, she watched his perfect smile reappear. Even as she drove away from the coffee shop, she couldn't stop thinking about him.

What had he done? Somehow, their brief interaction touched her heart. How could that be possible for a stranger to have her already overthinking her entire cup of coffee that developed into much more than a spill?

Chapter Five

DAYS AFTER THE coffee incident, the night of their dinner date finally arrived.

Truthfully, she hadn't really thought this would happen, that they would go out. She had been so busy with work the past week that it almost slipped her mind to make the plans. When she did think about it, even their first chance meeting, she attempted to dismiss it, not wanting another man to break her heart. Her heart had saddened deeply this past year and she just wanted to cope and move forward. Since a couple of days had passed, she thought surely Matt had forgotten about her. However, a sudden sweet text from him made it clear that he hadn't. That's when she really put her thoughts to where they should meet.

I hope your week is going well, and I look forward to our dining out sooner rather than later. Pick the place and time. I will be there. Rayleigh, I'm glad we happened to meet one another. Matt

Then a new challenge awaited her. It had been a long

time since a date task was on her, she had a hard time settling on a place.

The list of possible restaurants went on and on, and she was getting a headache from overthinking it. It didn't help that Alissa was making fun of her. Teasing her on her newfound romance when in fact it wasn't anything but a simple dinner.

Alissa enlightened her that this was not the first time Rayleigh had placed effort in planning or selecting a restaurant. She recounted the times Rayleigh had spent money on clothes and makeup, making sure they matched and looking the best she ever had. None of that had been good enough. For this date, she was planning to dress in what she already had and wearing only a hint of makeup. Alissa agreed less is better and she seemed to already like this Matt guy without meeting him yet, just from what Rayleigh had told her.

DATE NIGHT ARRIVED and her first surprise was that she happily scored a reservation with short notice for a popular eatery. She only phoned the place earlier in the day. Glad that perhaps someone cancelled, Rayleigh then sent a text to Matt of the time and place.

Her second surprise of the day was when the waiter led her toward her reserved table. Matt was already there. Not that her dates had ever been late. However, in most instances she was always the first one to arrive. She had made it a rule to be at least half an hour early. Sometimes, she had needed to wait to get a table since it wasn't ready yet.

This time, with Matt in her thoughts, she had forgotten that rule. She barely arrived on time. For the first time ever, she had to run through some yellow traffic lights, a few bordering on being red. What was usually a leisurely drive was a race against time. It was a wonder she wasn't panting and sweaty from how much she had rushed.

Letting herself get seated at the table, she immediately requested a glass of red wine—she needed something to calm her nerves. She turned her attention toward Matt. In this light, he looked remarkably handsome. His hair was swept up and he was wearing a greyish light blue sweater, which softened his deep colored eyes. The sweater fit his toned chest, and she noted that he definitely worked out. He appeared like he had some strength to him as well.

On the other hand, she felt severely underdressed. Apart from the restaurant, Matt's attire was so great that beside him, she felt like she wasn't dressed properly. Rayleigh glanced down at her casual black pants and simple printed blouse. No fancy high heels; she chose flats. Additionally, it didn't make it seem like she tried too hard to impress him with fashion. In fact, it would seem like she didn't try at all.

"Hi. You look wonderful," he said.

Rayleigh glanced at him in surprise; she couldn't help smiling. His eyes were shining as he studied her, flattering her immensely. Her unease immediately evaporated and she felt very comfortable in her chosen attire.

"Thank you. You look nice yourself. I like the color of your sweater."

"Oh, thanks. I tried to ditch the tie and shirt tonight, since I wear that daily."

The waiter approached their table with her glass of wine, temporarily breaking up their small talk. He explained the evening's specials and took a drink order from Matt. Then he told them he would be back to take their order.

Rayleigh felt Matt's eyes fixed on her the entire time the specials were outlined. She was excited being there with him. She secretly hid her blushing and content smile behind her menu. Her cheeks felt warm, and she was glad she hadn't applied too much blush earlier.

"I heard all the dinner selections the waiter told us but he missed one … you weren't listed," Matt stated playfully.

"Awww," she cooed. This was fun. Which was weird. She had never felt this much enjoyment before. Usually, at this point of time, she would be nearly stiff from nerves. "Thank you, that was sweet. After all I owe you a lot for putting up with my coffee mishap, tonight should go much better with no spills for me … for us."

"It'd be even better if I could keep my mouth shut. With a pretty girl seated so closely to me, I'm the one in '*Awww*' myself. I guess I wasn't supposed to tell you that," he said sullenly. He wanted to compliment her; he enjoyed seeing her smile.

The moment was interrupted to give the waiter their entrée selections. Matt was glad his drink—which was an

Old Fashioned of bourbon—arrived, because that would calm him, too. He was appearing very relaxed, but on the inside, he was hoping not to ruin this night with Rayleigh in any way. He had thought about her all week. Her gentle touch to his wet shirt that she immediately applied at the coffee shop. In fact, Matt had never been happier to have a ruined shirt.

With their orders placed, they began talking once more. Dinner went well after that. Matt noticeably engaged her to talk more about herself, and along the way he even elicited a couple of laughs from her.

She couldn't believe how great it was to talk to him. This was the most comfortable date she had ever had. She felt like she could be herself. She didn't feel the need to put on a front. The conversations progressed from topic to topic, flowing as easily as the coffee had. She had a wonderful time.

After dinner concluded, they exited the restaurant. Rayleigh's car was parked just a few spaces away. Her feet moved her toward her car, Matt by her side. They hadn't spoken about doing this again soon or said a good night to one another. They walked quietly together.

"What are you doing?" she questioned suspiciously, stopping a car away from her black Ford Escape.

"Walking you to your car?" he replied, his voice pitched higher at the end.

Placing her hands on her hips, she cocked her head to the side. "Are you asking me?"

"No. I mean, I'm walking you to your car. A gentleman always makes certain his date is safe."

"All right, so this was a date?" Rayleigh teased playfully.

"Yes, I believe it qualifies as that. And isn't that what a guy is supposed to do on a date? I didn't want to push asking if you want to come back to my place, but know that I would have offered that." Matt smiled sincerely.

"That's true. That's what a guy *is* supposed to do. Thank you for a nice evening, but I think I still owe you for how we first met."

"Look, Rayleigh, everything is fine. I just wanted to spend time with a beautiful woman, and I'm glad you said yes. I will take this as making it up to me."

"No," she replied. This wasn't enough. This was barely enough. He bought her a great dinner.

"All right. How about you stay with me a little longer?" He pulled her hand into his. "I am craving a little sweetness."

Rayleigh nodded, but then burst into laughter as she noticed his pull to a storefront serving ice cream. She lit up like a child.

"That sounds perfect. Let's go in. I love ice cream, and I know I won't spill it on you."

Chapter Six

THE NIGHT ENDED amicably. Rayleigh was able to return with a clear conscience. She had thoroughly enjoyed their time in the ice cream shop. The restaurant choice went quite well, and even full from dinner she made room to enjoy a small cup of mint chocolate chip hand-dipped ice cream. She watched closely as Matt's lips devoured a double scoop of chocolate marshmallow. Rayleigh was caught up in thinking what it would be like to kiss those sweet lips coated with chocolate. A few times her fingers swept away a drip of the ice cream that melted from his cone. The sweetness that he had shown her tonight—and not that from the sweet frozen treat—was a warming in her heart that she hadn't planned for.

Enough of Matt and our date night out. After all, they probably wouldn't be seeing each other anymore. This transaction was over. She had dinner to make up for ruining his shirt. This was the last time she was going to meet a man for a long time, or so she thought.

For now, she simply smiled each day, mostly thinking of how much fun she had that night with him. Nothing sexual, just talking and enjoying his company. Rayleigh had been her complete self that evening and it was refreshing. No attempts were made for her to impress him and she hadn't had to change herself in ways to accommodate a man that wouldn't do the same thing. That was the one thing she had taken away from that night. Matt was fun and made her smile more than she had in a long time.

She hadn't realized how much she had really changed in the past to please a man. The ways she had twisted and turned, going so far as bending over backwards to elicit a smile from them. Looking back, she had to wonder how desperate she had been. She paused, sure that Alissa would easily tell her she was pining over all the wrong men for years. Her pattern was that whenever a man came into her life, she would go headfirst and fall fast for them, but it's apparent none worked out.

Fortunately, she learned lessons along the way and heard it all, too—as Alissa had been the most vocal when rehashing all the men she shouldn't have dated. She seemed to finally leave her alone in the relationship conversation lately. Her friends also eased up on contacting her to come join them for evenings out or time at the lake. Her lifelong friends had given her space, and didn't involve themselves trying to fix her up with anyone, letting her be single and unattached for the time being. Rayleigh remained firm to herself this time, not jumping into having a boyfriend nor searching ever again on the internet for love.

However, Matt must not have gotten the feeling from her to steer clear. He wanted to pursue her. He sent her sweet messages. Often it was about something innocuous—like an article or a tweet about something he thought she would favor based on their initial conversations. They had talked a lot that night, and she had shared with him things she hadn't shared with most men. Recently, though, he had been asking to meet up with her again. Classifying it as a second date.

She was puzzled. After their parting from a delight of ice cream, she thought she had made her stance clear that they had a good time and thank you ... nothing more. She had even believed herself that would be their last time meeting each other.

She should be telling him no, but her heart told her she wanted to. Matt was inviting her for a sweet date of wine and chocolates. It was an upcoming convention he was hoping they would enjoy. Chocolates and wine got her attention, and that Matt was suggesting this. These all sounded pleasurable to her. It was something she could indulge in even with Matt ...

Her thoughts carried her to Matt and her having sex. She was certain he would be great in bed. Torn between hanging out another weekend in her apartment watching reruns and eating popcorn with extra butter with Alissa, or branching out to an enticing convention and seeing Matt again, Rayleigh found she was in a dilemma. This one, though, she had to go with the second date. Matt was the choice and Alissa would surely understand. For some reason Alissa hadn't met Matt, but was team Matt all the way.

"Oh, what's this?" Alissa asked, standing behind her desk chair as she read aloud the website page for the Sweet Wine convention. "An event for solely wine and chocolates. How can anyone resist that as they're letting you taste all the merchandise? Are you going? Rayleigh, you better go! It looks like a lot of fun, and with Matt, I think it will be awesome."

"I want to, and Matt seems nice. I'm just surprised you are in favor of this and not trying to squash it." Rayleigh groaned, pressing her head on her arm on the table. She tried to block the computer screen with her hair but the light penetrated through. Why was it the one time she needed her hair that it failed her?

"So, is that a yes?"

"It's a no." Sitting up, she glared resentfully at the screen. "Matt invited me to go with him. And while I want to go for the fun of the event and the chocolate, I think he will only let me down eventually and I don't want to deal with hurt again. Especially where my heart is concerned."

"He knows you. None of the other guys have ever done anything like this before," Alissa said in wonder. Rayleigh transferred her glare toward her roommate. Alissa held her hands up. "Don't look at me like that. It's simple … you wouldn't be agonizing over this date so much if you didn't really want to go."

"I know." Rayleigh blew out a breath. Then she turned her gaze to the ceiling. "All right. If I did go with him, would this count as a date?"

"Yes."

"Why?"

"You're not exactly friends. You shared with me that you met for dinner where he explicitly told you he wanted to be with you because you were beautiful. Matt paid for dinner and prolonged the evening with dessert on the spur of the moment, obviously not wanting you to leave or end the evening. And then you described to me that it was the absolute sweetest, lingering kiss he planted on your lips before you drove home. In fact, you didn't stop rubbing your lips when you came home from the date and even the next morning, I caught you doing it again. Nonchalantly you touched your lower lip over and over. I think you were yearning for his lips again." Alissa had a way of talking sense into Rayleigh. "I think Matt may be one of the good guys. I have a great feeling about him. I'm just trying to convince you to see it as I know you already feel it … it doesn't detract from the fact that he paid for dinner."

"Thanks for the detailed summary," she bit out. "Then I can easily go alone."

"You want to go alone? Sure. You can do that," Alissa suggested. "I can't go with you. I would if I could but I'm tied up this weekend."

"What if he's there, too? It's all weekend, maybe the day I go he won't be there. I can just say I have to work at the hospital."

"You want to lie to this man? Why would you do that?"

"I don't know what to do. He warmed my heart and I was getting used to it being cold. I think I'm afraid of the aftermath of getting let down. He seems to nice, too perfect."

"Lying isn't a sound foundation for any dating or potential relationship. I'm no one to give advice except I think he may be the one for you. I have a feeling. My hunches are usually right. Where you and I differ is I love hard, and also remove people from my life if I don't want to surround myself with them and I have no vague area. You, on the other hand, have always carried love for everyone from what I have seen, so much so that you haven't clued in on those that take advantage … perfect example was Roden."

"What? Why are you bringing his name up again? Ugh! I can't win. I understand you are looking out for me, Alissa. Once, before you and I lived together, I met a guy who I had strong feelings for. I had a sense he was cheating on me. I told him I had to go out of town and didn't. I watched him in the bar hit on another girl … they left together."

"Wow, you set him up and found out in your own detective work. I'm impressed," Alissa joked.

"Yeah, I did. We all have a past. I'm not too proud of it, lying and setting him up, but apart from the fact that I found him cheating on me. That was good to know before I actually planned my entire life with him. Don't tell me you have nothing you keep to yourself. I mean, I'm sure you do, but—"

"Well, there's the fact that I've chased away some of your dates before. I'm not ashamed of that. I'm proud that I protected you from those weirdos. When you care about someone you look after them as much as you can."

Rayleigh was shocked. This was the first time she'd heard about this. *Where's this coming from?* She also wondered who Alissa was speaking of, but if it was the past then it didn't matter right now. Her present was Matt. Before they got too far off the topic of the convention they were speaking of. Wine and chocolate. Rayleigh instantly thought of herself drinking a fine wine before having a chocolate massage. Her thoughts became delicious; suddenly, she envisioned Matt smoothing the warm chocolate onto her stomach and working his way lower.

"Rayleigh, are you listening to me? If you don't want to chance seeing Matt, then simply don't go."

"Where did you say to go?" Rayleigh responded, not paying attention to Alissa.

Alissa gave her a knowing look and her hastily erected defenses crumbled.

"Of course I want to go, and I will with him. If this falls apart, you, as my roommate, will hear all about it over and over, *I promise.*" Rayleigh emphasized the 'I promise.'

"Then go with him."

"Fine." Sitting up, Rayleigh sent the message. Then she looked at Alissa with angry eyes. "Why are you making me go out with him anyway? I thought you didn't like my dating choices."

"Well, he's different. I like him. He's going to be good for you. You'll see, trust me on this one."

"Whatever," she muttered. She hated how approving Alissa was being. Moving herself from their conversation and her desk chair, Rayleigh was now lying back in bed. She resolved to treat this like any other outing.

She wasn't going to dress to impress him at all. In fact, she was going to do her best to enjoy the weekend event and focus on the wine selection, immerse herself with sweets, and of course all in the company of Matt. Could he be the dream guy for her?

WAITING OUTSIDE IN the busy lobby of where the convention was taking place, Rayleigh found herself eager to go in. The rich scent of cocoa and sugar were wafting in the air and her mouth was salivating. Glancing impatiently at her watch, she returned to watching the crowd. He told her he'd be here by now.

Then she saw him pushing through the crowd. His face was red and sweat was dripping down his forehead from exertion. His shirt looked damp and was stuck to his body—not that she was complaining, because his muscles were highlighted nicely. However, that wasn't the point.

Why's he breathless and sweating so much?

"I'm so sorry," he said, stopping before her. She passed him a tissue to wipe himself with. His smile of gratitude lit up her heart.

"What happened? You look like you ran a marathon." Rayleigh's voice was laced with concern.

"My car broke down when I was making my way over

here. Then I had to wait at the side of the road until a tow truck came. By the time they towed my car into the shop, I realized I was running late. Initially, I would have been here early. Since the mechanic was close to this venue, I thought I should run here. It was only a few blocks."

"You ran here? In the middle of the day? With the sun right above the city, in all of its hot glory? Are you crazy? Wait here." She hurried away to get a bottle of water for him. There was no way she wasn't charmed by his efforts. She was smiling brightly. He ran here to meet her. He was appearing to be quite the keeper.

This time she wasn't running away, pushing away from him, but found herself wanting to tend to him. Care for him. Be with him.

Luckily, he looked much better when she returned. His face wasn't so red anymore and his breathing had slowed down. His eyes were warm and thankful when she gave him the bottled water.

Giving him space to recover, she excused herself to the ladies' room. Rayleigh tried to convince herself that she and Matt weren't here on a date. No matter what Alissa said, this was nothing more than friends attending an event. This was definitely not a date. However, earlier Rayleigh found herself taking a lot of time in selecting what to wear for her non date. She chose a simple, black button-up shirt and jeans; low, kitten-heeled black boots, and a light fabric infinity scarf with black, tan, and a hint of raspberry colors.

THIS DAY COULDN'T get sweeter. As soon as they entered the venue, Rayleigh was in sugar heaven. Most nights at the hospital she relied on a caffeine drink to boost her energy or any chocolate bar from the vending machines. Good thing her metabolism burned off the extra calories.

Matt smiled, watching her transform suddenly to a youthful kid in a candy shop who had just been given free rein. She eagerly went table to table, sampling the various wines, and sharing the delights that melted in her mouth with Matt.

Everything tasted so good. She wanted to eat more, but her stomach protested the sudden influx of alcohol and sugar. Grumbling fiercely, she hurriedly chucked the remaining chocolate truffle in Matt's mouth before clutching her abdomen tightly.

This was bad. This day was turning sour quickly.

Allowing Matt to swiftly steer her out, she was overcome with sickness and had no idea what was going on. Not caring about anything that was happening around her, she continued to hold onto him. Feeling ill, she didn't want to be alone.

However, she needed to try to muster up the strength to hold back and not be so clingy. She had told herself she didn't need a man or a relationship to be happy. She just needed herself. That crutches were not allowed. If she did this, it was a slippery slope back down to needing a man that she would lose herself to, and with time, inevitably be back alone, kicking herself again for falling too fast for a man.

No, she could do this on her own. She didn't need anyone. She had thrown herself into far too many sips of wine combined with decadent treats. She was the one who had to deal with the consequences. No matter how painful those were … and her body was feeling quite bad. Matt led her to the sitting area, and she watched him head to the bar. Within a moment she was sliding into the comfy chair in the vast hotel lobby. She bent over herself, resting her forehead on her knees. *This is so bad*, she thought, embarrassed at how this must look to Matt. Then again, if she wasn't on a date, she shouldn't care that much about him and more about her current condition.

"Here. Take some of this." Matt gave her a glass of ginger ale. "Sip some and see if it calms your stomach. This used to work for me."

Confused, she lifted her gaze and saw that it was Matt comforting her. He was dutifully taking care of her, and the thing that caught her attention was his compassionate and genuine expression. There was a deeply concerned, worried look in his eyes. It was different from those who were concerned for formality's sake.

"Here," he said, opening the bottle he held and pouring a bit more after she had taken a few sips. She wasn't able to do anything else but take it. *Why is he doing this?* "I asked at the bar for something to help settle your sudden upset stomach. I don't know if it will work as you got a bit of everything mixed together inside of you."

A bit of everything? What does he mean?

Looking downward, she could only imagine the sugar shock and washing it down with wine and more wine. She reminded herself she hadn't eaten earlier in the day so the mix of all the convention displays took a toll on her. Her own question was answered when she felt her stomach rumble, probably bulging from all she consumed. At least she enjoyed the venue initially. After sitting there and polishing off the rest of the drink he held for her, Rayleigh's stomach was feeling much better.

"Thank you—Matt, stop." She was appreciative, but looking to the side, she pushed his hand away from pouring her a refill. He seemed uncertain but acceded to her request. She was glad. More so happy she hadn't gotten sick and thrown up. That would be more embarrassing than her current state. "I'm feeling a bit better. Wow, that hit me really quick."

"Glad I was with you. Are you sure you're okay?" he responded with a smile but she could see he wasn't placated. He looked like he wanted to try a different remedy.

"I'm fine now. I just ate a bit too much chocolate, too fast, followed by wine chasers. Not a good combination. I mean, I liked it all but overindulged, you think?"

He grinned. "Maybe just a bit."

"I'm sure. If I head home and rest for a couple of hours and I'll be as good as new."

"All right. All right. I get it," he said, letting out a breath.

She appreciated his show of concern. He was definitely worming his way into her heart. There was a noticeable change in the expression on his face, suddenly making her wary.

"What?" she questioned to gather the reason for his disappointment in his eyes.

"I, um, I wanted to invite you out to dinner after this fun day together, but—"

"Matt, you know I only agreed to this event as friends, right?" she asked, hating she had to reject him. That was what she had told him before agreeing. It was unfair for him to change the rules on the fly, suddenly wanting to add more time with her.

There really is no crime in that, Rayleigh thought, and perhaps she needed to let go and feel what she was almost unable to contain around him anymore. Her heart was alive with his presence. She felt like she disappointed him with feeling sick and cutting off his gesture of spending more time with her.

"I know that's all you wanted, Rayleigh, but I have to be honest … when I saw you again, I realized that I really like you. I can't let this opportunity slide."

"But—"

"I know you have your reservations, but I just want the chance for you to get to know me better. Please just give me that much … a chance."

Later, she'd remind herself that his plea was heard echoing within the lobby walls and the crowd that had formed in the lobby to enter the venue was now looking their way, enjoying their romantic performance. So, she had agreed to make him stop. That wasn't wrong. Technically, she gave in for the moment just because his pleading was so genuine and sweet. Not that she hadn't had plenty of sweets for the day. Where Matt was concerned, she knew he was peeling away her layers of the wall she was surrounding herself in. One layer at a time was coming down, and despite her efforts she was not going to continue to fight him.

In her heart of hearts, she knew she wanted to go out with him. He was already better than most of the other men she dated. It was just a matter of learning more about him.

Hopefully, she wouldn't fall into being blindsided with hopes and dreams like those that had gripped her with Roden.

Chapter Seven

AFTER THEIR SECOND date—which started well and ended sickening—Rayleigh and Matt were officially dating. They didn't necessarily go on many dates. Their work and schedules didn't match the majority of the time. However, they talked over the phone a lot. That was where she learned the most about him and vice versa.

As much as she liked being around him, the phone calls sounded so much more intimate. With his voice drifting into her ears, it was like he was right beside her. She felt very comfortable then. She could divulge many of her worries and secrets over the phone.

Thinking about it, it was embarrassing how much she had told him. No topics were off limits, especially for her. She told him about her ex-lovers, her friends. Even though she was still licking her wound, she had told him about the Roden incident, too.

That had been rough. This was the first time she had opened up about this with anyone else apart from Alissa. It was great. He sounded so understanding. He even said that he would take things slow. Her stony heart was chipped away slowly but surely.

Alissa looked happy for her. She still teased Rayleigh about her weak resolve, but Rayleigh could tell she was genuinely happy. She was glad that she got her approval. No one had gotten that from Alissa; she had a firm opinion on whom Rayleigh dated. It felt like an achievement now that she finally agreed on Matt and watched Rayleigh enjoy more time spent living and loving with him, not wallowing in their apartment.

Though many times she spoke of things from her heart, she never came to deal with the loss of life that appeared before her that evening months back while on her hospital rotation. Somewhere deep in her soul she stored the sorrow. Rayleigh didn't think anyone could bring that out of her nor was she ready to cope with someone younger than her passing. Someone who was lively and outspoken—perhaps sometimes too outspoken, but one who stood at Ridge Rock Lake smiling at what a fun-filled day it would be. Until it was tragically cut short … forever. Rayleigh rubbed her eyes to prevent the well of tears that formed, not wanting that dam to break again. Swallowing hard, she held it at bay.

Alissa caught her tender moment. "Rayleigh, are you okay?"

"I will be … I keep remembering one horrible day. I wish I could turn back time."

"We all wish that, just be thankful for the moments you treasured. Don't count the time, recant the good experience," Alissa offered comforting words.

"Thank you. When did you get so wise?" Rayleigh attempted to laugh, and her tears fell hard. *Happy tears*, she tried to claim. They were for a time spent long ago, time she would never get again unless in heaven one day.

THE MONTHS PASSED by, and Matt and Rayleigh continued their developing relationship. Matt was a counselor for what Rayleigh assumed was a school or classes. He didn't confide much on the cases he worked on or individuals. She knew where the building was that his office was in, and it was near the high school, so her assumption was that they were connected, the school and his employment.

Their times on the phone were much longer now. Before, a half hour was sufficient. Now, they could spend an hour or two. He liked to tell her about anything interesting that happened. For Rayleigh, hearing him relay a story to her, she was very interested to know what he found noteworthy.

Sometimes, it was as simple as running into an old friend, other times, it could be about an insight at how different people were and how that could be explained. For some reason, she preferred the latter because it made her really appreciate his depth. He always spoke to her with reason and listened. Never did he just agree and not hear her words. Often, he would elaborate on something they talked about prior. She knew then he had heard her.

Through it all, Alissa continually teased her. Sometimes, she would even disturb her when she was on the phone. That was frustrating as Rayleigh hadn't told Matt anything about Alissa. Not even mention that she had a roommate. One day she would introduce them. Especially since Alissa had nothing but greatness formed for him already.

MATT PHONED HER late this evening, sounding serious and uncertain. That caught Rayleigh's attention. They had been speaking on the phone for the past hour and it was getting late. Glancing at the time, she realized she should go to bed soon. However, Matt sounded like he had something to say.

"Matt? Is everything all right?" she asked when the silence wore on. She had even looked at the screen of her phone to make sure the call was still active.

"Yeah. I just don't know how to say this."

"Just say it. If it's something I can help with, I'd be more than happy."

"It's going to make you mad."

"Really?" She was intrigued. "Lay it on me."

"Are you seeing somebody?"

"What are you talking about? I'm seeing you."

"I mean … I know that, but what I mean is … ugh, there's not a good way to say this. I don't want to ask, and I know the answer, but—"

"Are you asking if I'm seeing someone behind your back?" she asked incredulously, her voice high-pitched.

"Yes. Exactly. That's right. That's the question I need an answer to."

"I can't believe this. I'm hanging up—"

"Wait!" he shouted, nearly deafening her. She was offended but her curiosity compelled her to hear him out. "Wait. I know it sounds bad, which is why I didn't want to ask the question, but I need to know."

"I'm not seeing anyone else. There's only you. Which is a misnomer since I haven't actually seen you in about a week." Tears began spilling down Rayleigh's cheeks; she was clearly upset.

Matt must have heard hear sniffle because he was scrambling to recover. "I know. I know. Look, don't cry. I trust you. I really do."

"Then why did you even ask this?"

"Because I keep hearing you talking to someone in the background."

She stilled. He must have heard her talking to Alissa. Earlier on, she told him she lived alone—no need to elaborate that she shared her apartment with Alissa. So, Matt was wise to question who she was speaking with while talking to him.

"I mean, I know you don't have a roommate. You would have mentioned if you had a friend staying over. So, I got to thinking—"

"I'm just talking to myself," she lied, playing it off with a weak laugh.

"Wha—"

"Sometimes I have weird thoughts in my head. It's so weird that I almost want to say it out loud. That was what the 'talking' is about." She couldn't believe the words coming out of her own mouth, trying to reassure Matt. It was so ridiculous her scrambling to tell him something. No one would believe this.

"Oh. That makes sense."

He believes me? She was shocked. He was usually so sharp during their talks. This passed right over.

"Thanks for understanding. I didn't want to say anything because it's weird and all."

"It's all right. I suppose I was worried for nothing."

"I'm glad you asked me about it. I don't want things between us to turn badly. I care about you, Matt. I'm happy you're in my life."

"It's nothing actually, Rayleigh. I just questioned it when you seemed to be carrying on another conversation when you told me to hold on for a moment. The other conversation I overheard you sounded incredibly comfortable with someone to argue with them. It's not much but that really got me thinking."

Wow. He got that from a few snippets of overhearing a background conversation? He was good. The conversation between her and Matt veered on a safe path soon after and they were able to end their call amicably and express they missed one another.

Even after that, she believed she still couldn't get the conversation he overheard out of his head.

She didn't want him to have doubts about her. Maybe she should simply tell him the truth. What was the truth though? If she confessed to him it would hurt their relationship. Rayleigh debated what to do. He was such a kind, perfect man. She didn't want to ruin what they were becoming, but she had to come clean with him. Perhaps she would when the timing was right.

Chapter Eight

I F IT MEANT seeing him face-to-face, she would, and somehow hope things were still really great between them. Driving into the parking lot, Rayleigh couldn't believe she was going to drop in on her boyfriend at his job. This was the worst way to talk to him about the insights he questioned. She couldn't help it. She had been swamped with working hospital shifts and couldn't even take a day off until this new week. The only reason she was able to do this was because she's off for the next two days and an errand happened to take her close to his office.

Luckily, she already had the address of his work. It wasn't anything odd her dropping in—he asked her a week ago to remember to drop his briefcase off next time they got together, he left it in her car the last date they were on. Knowing his work papers were contained in there she thought this was as good of a chance to pop in on him and also get his work items back to him should he be needing them. She hadn't thought any deeper into anything other than this being a simple, quick visit.

Once parked, she made her way to the building where his car was in the front spot. Bountiful flower pots were placed at the entrance doors. Rayleigh could smell the floral fragrance as she walked closer. There were two white painted wood benches on both sides of the pavement for outdoor seating. A quaint office seating, it seemed so peaceful. When she looked at the two-story red brick structure clearer, it suddenly became alarming. She wished she turned around and got back to her car and drove off quickly. There was a sign right beside the entrance door in black raised letters. It read the words she dreaded. It said "Parkside Centre for Grief Counselling".

Her stomach immediately dropped. She felt sickness wash over her. Rayleigh wanted to leave and wished for her feet to get her to quickly run away. Every facet of her rejected what it said and what it stood for. She wasn't ready to face this. However, the opportunity to do that was lost when she heard her name being called out from behind.

"Rayleigh, what are you doing here?" Matt asked, coming over from the adjacent building. Any illusions she might have were gone. He had just confirmed her suspicions. As much as she wanted to reject his arms, protest his occupation … she couldn't.

She had missed him. It had been days since they had seen each other. Wrapping her arms around him, she sniffed in his comfortable scent and tears sprang to her eyes. As much as she tried to hold back, the tears began falling and her nose ran and she attempted to sniffle it away.

"Rayleigh? What's going on?" he asked, trying to break her hold and look at her.

Rayleigh tightened her arms around him. She didn't want him to see her when she was like this—distraught with tears running down her face.

Inevitably, he did see it. He led her into the building where he worked, and into his office where he watched her grieving, sad eyes raise toward his. Tenderly, he helped her get seated on the couch, hearing her continued, uncontrolled sniffles. Grabbing the tissues he held out, she turned away to fix her face. Then when she was sure her eyes were dry, she turned back to him.

"Is everything all right?" he asked, sitting across from her.

"Y-Yeah. I just missed you so much," she said, her voice still thick with tears.

He came to sit beside her and hugged her close. "Me too. I wanted to rush over to your place the other night to apologize after I questioned you, that was tough not to. Then this week, so much work has piled up, and you were busy, too."

"I know."

"But I don't think that's the true reason for all these tears. I would love to think you missed me that much ..."

"W-What are you talking about?"

"I observed that you began crying even before seeing me. I watched your tears fall right here, outside of the building. You were crying looking up toward the sign hanging on the brick. What is this about? You don't like my line of work? Wait … Rayleigh, are you struggling through grief yourself?" Matt tuned it to her reaction to his place of employment, now recognized her sudden unhappiness.

Even though she knew he was talking in jest at first, she couldn't say anything to refute him. She was grieving. Even months after her sister's death, she still hadn't gotten used to her not being there. Rayleigh at first shut out the world with her loss, then to get herself through day to day, she had to come up with this illusion to feel that Alissa was still present.

"Y-You are. Rayleigh, I can see the sadness in your eyes. You have had a relative or loved one who passed away."

"Yes. I suffered a horrible loss, a part of me that is gone. It was a sudden, tragic death. She was my twin sister, Alissa. Most knew her as Monroe, a nickname she took on early in her teen years, she thought it was a cool. She and I were tied closer than just a name, we were fraternal twins. Didn't look alike, nor act similarly, but our hearts were connected that same day we were both born." Rayleigh clutched her stomach, the hurt still stirring within. However, it was a relief to finally talk about it with someone, but more so with him.

"I didn't know you had a twin. I didn't know she passed. You never shared that with me. I'm here for you now if you want to talk about her or anything. Rayleigh, you can lean on me."

"I guess I want to share it, I don't know. Since she died, I've been seeing her around. I actually visualize her walking about my apartment like she never left. She's still poking her nose in my life. She even comes around to tease and disturb me. I've actually reclaimed her as my imaginary roommate. I feel such comfort keeping her alive in my mind." Rayleigh's eyes reddened. She swept away the tears that clung to her cheek.

"She's the one you were speaking with that night we talked on the phone? You were carrying on two conversations, ours and with her, right? That makes sense now."

"You sounded like you didn't believe the 'talking to myself' response I gave you. Matt, I hated to lie to you like that, but I feel she is so real in my daily life most of the time."

"While many people suffer from it, I didn't think you had that problem yourself. This all makes perfect sense," Matt offered.

She appreciated his understanding. Matt held her hand and rubbed her back, offering comfort as she opened up to him about that tragic day that Alissa was taken from her life. It was a slight relief to her chest and heart to open up to someone after all this time. She hadn't been able to talk about it with anyone else.

"I had been with her earlier in the day at the lake. She was beautiful in her black bikini, ready to dive into the lake for a swim. It was one she had borrowed from my dresser drawer, but it looked better on her. I remember her tipping her sunglasses down, giving me a glance and a fake frown with her lips, playing up the part to keep me there and miss going into work. Although she tried to persuade me to remain, I had to leave. Now, I wish I had stayed. Maybe she and I would have swam enough that she would have not partaken in jumping off the old bridge to her death. Imagine the impact I felt to see her arrive at the hospital, my workplace, dead. Her body unresponsive. Leaving me with not a final word, no hug, just instantly gone." Rayleigh paused. "I laid on my living room floor for days, not wanting to rise to a new day. It took me months to get a routine again. I think I turned my grief to a creative way of not facing her forever departure." Rayleigh glanced toward Matt, seeking his understanding.

"You have been through so much; the question is what do you want to do now?"

"What do you mean?" she questioned, her brow furrowed in confusion.

"Well, I work in grief counseling, and I can help you with this. But you're my girlfriend, so I'm not sure I'm really up for the job. My heart is fully vested in you."

"I don't want to do anything about this per se."

"All right, I won't bother you about it—"

"But I do want to resolve it. If you can recommend me a counselor, I think I can talk more about it, I would like to try," she stated. Rayleigh needed an outlet for all her grief and constant made-up interaction with her sister. She resolved that she would love to not be haunted by her everyday in her mind.

"Rayleigh, you will get through this. In fact, each new day may get better. I will find someone who can help you more than I can. Know I am here for you as well."

Chapter Nine

MATT WORKED HARD to find a counselor for her. He would do anything for Rayleigh and only wanted to see her smiling once more. Matt had gone around interviewing his colleagues to get the best fit. While she had appreciated his efforts before, she was really touched at how far he was willing to go. When she asked him about it, he had waved away her gratefulness.

"You're my girlfriend. If I won't do this for you, who else am I supposed to do it for?"

That just made her cry.

Matt's efforts continued to impress her. He would even meet her during her counseling days. Waiting for her session to end to embrace her in his arms and offer strength for her to continue moving forward. For so long he didn't know she was stuck in grief, in a make-believe world of still having her twin nearby. The loss of a loved one is profound and no one has the manual of how to act or react. His heart saddened knowing the ache she had been carrying alone.

OVER THE NEXT few weeks, Rayleigh was getting the help she needed to cope and could see the effects of her counseling working. Where before Alissa would bother her most every day, she would appear less often each day. That made her sad, as it felt like a second good-bye. In a way, she had time to really bade farewell to her best friend, her soul mate, her twin.

Then there came that one day of nothing but silence. Alissa didn't appear at all. Rayleigh decided to take her relationship with Matt to the next level and didn't receive any comments from Alissa nor any heated debates. Her silence led Rayleigh to believe she was positively progressing with her life and her new relationship.

MAKING THE FINAL preparations, she lit many various size candles and the room had a warm glow. A wine bucket on the table held a chilled bottle of bubbly if they wanted pop that open. She prepared a small charcuterie for them to consume. Mainly, she wanted him to taste her lips and satisfy her cravings for the feelings her brought out in her. Rayleigh rushed to the door when the bell rang. Her heart was beating so fast. She was so nervous. She hadn't done this in a long time, and was afraid that she had forgotten about everything. Seducing a man was a work of art and she didn't want to blow it.

"Come in," she said, waving her hand to enter her apartment.

"Thanks. What's the occasion?" Matt asked when he saw the candles and the dim lights setting up a scene for romance.

"It's just I'm ready to take this to the next level, us to another level," she blurted out. She wanted to bang her head on the wall. There went her plan to be subtle. Hoping she hadn't scared him off, she looked at him and was surprised at how still he was.

"When you say next level, you mean up those stairs to your bedroom for sex, right?"

"Y-Yes."

"Are you sure?"

"Yes."

"What brought this about?"

"I'm slowly getting over Alissa. I haven't seen her at all today. So, I want to celebrate the silence in my head. It's a step forward for me after these past months. The funny thing is thoughts of you have filled it all day."

"Rayleigh, help me understand … what does not having heard from Alissa have anything to do with sleeping with me?"

"Oh, Matt. Look, I just want to be with the man I love. Is that so—Uhm," she let out a yelp when he suddenly pulled her into his arms. Then his mouth covered hers in a hot, wet kiss. Her yelp turned into a groan.

Why did I hold out for so long? He was incredibly good. Grabbing the back of his head, she pulled him closer for a deeper kiss. Hooking her legs over his hips, their entwined bodies lowered down onto her couch. He barely noticed as he yanked her shirt over her head and kissed her neck.

"I've been holding back," he whispered as his hand burrowed into her jeans. She let out a hiss when he found her already wet for him. Then he roughly pulled her jeans and pale blue silk panties down while looking apologetically down at her. "I'm sorry, Rayleigh. I can't stop myself. It'll be better next time. I promise. I just want you so bad … right now."

As he said that, he plunged into her depths. It felt terrific. It had been a while for her as well. Wrapping her arms around his shoulders, she unconsciously bit into him when he hit a good spot.

It didn't take her long to reach her peak. As stars exploded behind her eyes, she felt him stiffen and then shake with one final thrust. Then they dropped to the gray fabric couch tired and spent as her many throw pillows were pushed to the hardwood flooring. Oddly enough, they never made it to her upstairs bedroom. Rayleigh was certain that Alissa would have given her full approval for the sexual explosion that took place in the living room.

WHAT A GREAT time they shared last night. Wearing a huge smile on her face, Rayleigh approached the morning beaming. She was already up and waiting for Matt to come back over. He didn't spend the night, but that didn't stop them from having another tryst in her bed before he left. After last night, it all became clear to Rayleigh what her next step would be. She shared her loving thoughts and wishes with Matt. Rayleigh was relieved as his response was an intense, warm embrace and a very passionate kiss.

Eagerly she greeted Matt at her apartment door. Her lips offered him a quick kiss on the cheek. Matt looked so handsome with his sport coat, tee shirt, and jeans. Rayleigh grabbed her denim jacket from the closet and put it on over her simple white shirt. She was also wearing jeans today for the plans they had. Not letting Matt enter beyond the threshold, she grabbed his hand and off they went.

"Are you ready?" Matt asked.

Rayleigh tightened her grasp on his hand. "As ready as I have ever been."

"Then let's do this." Matt tugged her along toward his car.

After Matt drove a short distance, they both arrived to where they decided to spend the afternoon. At first Rayleigh sensed they were not alone. That was perfectly okay because today was designated to be her release day. Not toward love for Matt—that was already sealed last night—but to let her twin sister, Alissa, go.

The autumn air was not too cool; a slight breeze moved the remaining leaves on the trees. Lying back on the dead, thick straw that was months ago green, fresh grass, Rayleigh felt so alive. Great long forgotten memories poured in her head. This day and this place were so special. Matt and her planned to come to this park. It was the one Alissa so loved to fly kites at long ago. Matt and Rayleigh held onto the huge, bright pink balloon that Matt earlier picked up from the party store before he arrived at Rayleigh's apartment. Last night as they came together, they also shared time with their bodies separated and conversed. While they spoke, they came up with their plans for today. It was now time for Alissa to rise to the heaven above, and not be held here anymore. Looking up at the balloon slightly swaying back and forth, Rayleigh's eyes followed its movement.

"Matt, this is love worth holding onto, and I have carried her in my heart, my apartment, and mind for months. I now believe I can let her go. I will never forget her, through the good and bad, happy and sad." Rayleigh paused.

"Rayleigh, know that you will always have her near. What you are doing now is helping yourself to let go, and as this balloon carries itself to the skies above, I will remain by your side, sending Alissa love and letting her know that you now and forever will have me to hold onto and carry in your heart as you have her."

"It's just so hard … we were twin sisters. We played, fought, dressed up and down together. Took our first steps, first words, first tears and laughs all with one another. Despite any distance from her, when one sister would fall, or get injured, the other hit the ground too with pain and sorrow. That night months ago when my friends called me at the hospital, I heard the sadness carried in their tone that Alissa was being transported to the hospital where I was doing my clinical rotation. When I saw her lifeless body arrive, all I could mutter to myself as pain ripped through my heart in the emergency room was, 'She's gone, Alissa has left my world.' I didn't want that to be true, I didn't get a chance to say good-bye, or tell her so many things. I knew then I would never see her carefree personality reign again around me or within our group of friends." Rayleigh was hesitating in her words. Emotion gripped hold of her.

Matt learned in his years of grief counseling to listen and let those going through this hard time. Their release of words may help them heal a bit better in time.

As they both laid there, gazing at the sky, a few puffy white clouds skirted past and then cleared allowing a solid blue backdrop to present itself.

"Matt, you are the reason I'm here to launch this balloon. Let it fly, let my sister take off peacefully from my imagination that carried her and comforted me yet also pained me so these past months."

"I did nothing, you decided it was time. I only want to help you wherever and whenever I can," Matt offered his comforting words.

"You have done more than you know. For so long I tried to fill a void in my heart with wanting a quick relationship. Then, when that failed, I turned that theory to warding men off and staying in my sad life of mostly communicating with Alissa who wasn't even real. Truth is I hurt more than I ever displayed. I have learned it's okay to break apart and cry. I don't regret keeping her memory and her alive with me all this time. If anything, I think she had a part in our coming together like it was her final task her on Earth."

"Rayleigh, you have come so far without even seeing it in yourself."

"I believe I have, too. I have gained strength I didn't know I had and resolve from this situation. It's life, basically, which is sometimes so happy and then also other times so devastatingly challenging."

Matt had been holding the balloon but looked at Rayleigh, and she nodded as if telling him she was ready for him to hand it over to her. Gently he passed it to her and noticed she had possession of it with the string secured within her fingers.

"Matt, I know just as I loved her and still do, that the love between you and I is worth holding onto. I love you." Rayleigh teared up.

As she reached to wipe her forming tears, the balloon slipped through her open fingers. The balloon took off in flight to soar across the sky and to wherever it was carried. Instead of panic to retrieve the string and hold onto the balloon, for the first time Rayleigh felt at peace and a sigh of relief overcame her. As it floated upward, her blue eyes brightened and followed the pink dot in the sky until she could see it no more. Her eyes closed and Matt pulled her into his arms. They laid there for what seemed forever. Rayleigh knew that for the rest of her life if she saw a pink balloon it would be a sign to her that Alissa was near. For that happy thought alone, she smiled. Almost immediately her content lips parted to welcome a sweet, tender kiss from Matt.

Life's good, she thought. We all try to hold on and not let go, but sometimes we find that one person to lean on—only Rayleigh fell in love along way and she knew Alissa was smiling down on her for that and would continue to.

In the soft breeze, Rayleigh almost thought she heard Alissa tell her, *"I told you so. He's the one. I approve. You'll do just fine without me. I will, though, be watching you from above … forevermore. I may have left you far too early but we will always be connected in our hearts. We* are *sisters, not* were *sisters."*

RAYLEIGH SLEPT PEACEFULLY that evening spooning with Matt in her bed. She dreamt of Alissa for the first time and chuckled in her dream state. Alissa was all dressed up in a white, tight-fitting dress with silver high heels. It made her taller than Rayleigh recalled, but then again, her twin mostly wore flats.

"Why are you dressed so prissy and pretty? What's the special occasion?" Rayleigh asked in her mind.

"I'm not prissy, I just tried to dress up girlie like you. Maybe I will

wear this on your wedding day when you marry Matt. I'm sure you have thought of that already … and if not, that's why I am here to pop into your thoughts and plant that seed. I can wear white the same day. After all, no one will see me. Sis, I would rather be in faded, ripped jeans and a black tank top, but for you I thought I would dress up one last time. Enjoy your dream and many more to follow. I'll drop in here and there until we meet again." Alissa smiled toward Rayleigh happily. Bright white illuminated behind her, blending into her dress.

Rayleigh tried to keep her in focus if she could, just like the bright pink balloon, until Alissa completely faded away. A trace of silver was her last vision. There was no sadness this time for Rayleigh because she looked forward to the next sign or dream with her sister appearing and warming her heart once more. In her mind, she would never let Alissa go.

The End

Although never an ending when you forever remember a loved one.

Heartfelt Remembrance

If roses grow in Heaven, please pick a bunch for me.
Gently lay them in my sister's arms and tell her they're from
    me.

Let the delicate flowers be a sign to let her know that I love
    her and will miss her.

We often don't get the chance for the final good-bye.
A loved one, though despite many ups and downs,
will always remain heartfelt as long as another heart beats
    here on Earth.

If roses grow in Heaven, please pick a bunch for me.
I will keep love in my heart for those who have fallen too
    early,
and they will never be forgotten by me.

Love, Renee xo

Renee Lee Fisher
USA TODAY BESTSELLING AUTHOR
Contemporary Romance

An Author that has the passion for putting her pen and ideas to paper. A pure romance junkie and she loves to tell stories. Renee continues pushing forward with her creativity.

Currently she is finishing up THE HEARTBEAT SERIES which are Contemporary Rock Romance Novels titled (ROCK NOTES, LOVE NOTES, MUSIC NOTES, FIRST BEAT, FIRST BASS and FIRST TASTE).

THERE IS A CD titled "SIMPLY MAD" with lyrics written from within The Heartbeat Series by Renee Lee Fisher that is LIVE on several music platforms worldwide.

THE CROSSING SERIES: THE KNOT HOLE, THE PASSAGE and THE MUSE are time traveling romance stories that will take you on an endearing romantic tale from the present day to the past.

DERAILED is a standalone romance. Love changes everything in this sweet romantic suspense.

Don't look for Renee to stop writing anytime soon, she is like the Duracell Bunny that keeps going and going. She is said to only sleep four hours a night and continues to create many more story lines for the readers to enjoy.

Renee resides in Eagleville, PA. with her husband Michael, of many years and her cats – Nyah, Leo and Lincoln. She has a great support system of Love from her family, friends and wonderful Street Team – The Vivacious Vixens.

Renee BELIEVES you should follow your DREAMS and that,
The HAPPIEST of people don't have the best of everything, they simply make the best of everything.

Renee loves to travel, especially to St. Martin – Netherland Antilles. She enjoys meeting new people to inspire her and she will always write down a person's name that is unique to use as a potential character in her future writings.

Excerpt from Rock Notes

Chapter One – Meeting

I AM IN A NEW part of my life, driving through an early spring day, air thick with falling petals swirling about. I think back to where I was months ago and I remember my marriage ending. It was a horrible cycle of emotions for me, first came so many tears and pain. Then I had so many questions as to why was I suddenly replaced with a woman that he hired to work in his office. I thought we had a solid and secure relationship. His walking away from me was staggering. I then suffered loss of self esteem and later I found anger which was hard for me to release, I kept so much inside. I still carry with me a self-doubt. I'm not sure I can rely on my judgment enough to trust any future partner. My husband ending our marriage knocked me down, but each new road I travel, I will get stronger. I turn on the radio to hear something to sway my mood. The music immediately takes me away on a journey as I travel briefly from traffic light to traffic light through town. Seems like the changing of the light pattern is in a sequence of musical themes like the chorus repeating over and over, red – yellow – green. Go – it is now time for me to go and begin my journey writing about the band. Conveying through my words their passion, their singing, and their *playing to becoming seasoned musicians. I follow all the traffic to the concert this evening.*

This is my story **Rock Notes**.

"MAX, MAX, MAX RAND EXCUSE me, do you have a moment to talk to me?" I closed in on the far corner of the stage. I had purchased a front row ticket to this evening's local concert to take in tunes and set myself up for the possibility of conversation. "I know you don't know who I am so let me introduce myself. I am Madison Tierney, call me Madison or Maddy. I am a freelance creative writer, once a columnist and now I'm writing a book titled, "Rock Notes" which I follow a band in depth, and I'd like that to be your band "Rolling Isaac's." I didn't want to intrude on his time, so I simply said, "I know you have so many young ladies wanting you to sign autographs and their bodies," I smiled and continued to talk in a confident manner, "but I just wanted to give you my business card in case we can speak in the near future or have your band representation contact me."

Looking up at Max and his combination of youthful and mature yet awesome, truly awesome good looks, I shouted out "Oh and I thought the show was great." I beamed about it trying to remain calm, as I was more mature, rather than getting all flustered by a mere young band playing.

Max looked me over from his vantage point above and smiled a kind brim and nodded. I drank in all his chiseled features and his dark chocolate, delicious hair that had tousled all over during the concert, looking very sexy like he had been rolling in bed for hours. It was then that he turned slightly to jump down and he placed his stunning, well built arms on the edge of the stage and the tattoo under his sleeve peeked briefly through. He was wearing a tight white long sleeve tee pushed up onto his forearms, and he was completely soaked with his sweet sweat from singing to the crowd. I wasn't certain what was inked on him but I knew it drew me in. It was colorful and his tee shirt sleeve was stuck to him. I could see his firm, fit stomach also as the tee clung to his torso. I looked up, startled to see he was now standing in front of me and still smiling tenderly. He took my hand gently and slightly slid his finger over my fingertip as sensation ran through me, it was only for him to take the business card but it left me sort of out of breath, scattered my thoughts for a moment. His eyes pulled me in like an inviting Caribbean ocean, they were a deep tropical blue and his dark eyelashes swept over them. I had to rethink and tell my body to blink as I was captivated. I thanked him and hoped to hear from him and as he walked back I stood and stared at his tall frame and truly awesome body…he did not turn around. I went to finally leave when my feet would allow me to move them and I glanced back to take in the entire empty, darkened stage only to see him leaning on the far side and sending a smile and wink my way. I looked around to see if it was meant for someone else and then back to him where he laughed and nodded his head to me.

I walked to my car and thought about Max Rand and our brief meeting and I was concerned about my attire for some odd reason…as it took me hours to decide earlier what to put together which was very unlike me. It was like taking time to prep for a date. I kept reselecting pieces from my closet to make me look a bit more hip and trendy. Finally I had chosen simple jeans, black boots and a black top with open shoulder areas. The appliqué on the shirt was a striking detailed cross with hearts that seemed to dance across the top and wrap to the back, almost like a hug, I added a black gem belt. Checking my look in the mirror, I was content and headed to the concert. I was just about to take hold of the car handle when my cell phone sounded, its timing making me think I set off my car alarm. I reached into my pocket and was surprised to read:

I watched your nervous smile, and caught a glimpse of the top you wore, one of my inks looks like it. I sing yes, but I am also believe it or not, involved in the band's representation…can we continue our conversation at a quiet space tomorrow? Max Rand

I fumbled for a reply to him, could this actually be happening, he was contacting me in mere moments? I sent him a voice text as a reply –

Yes, sure. Under my breath I said absolutely.

That was so stupid of me, an adult to say yes, sure, and he probably heard me say absolutely…what was I thinking, I had to be in control of this proposal for my writing and I should not feel like a school girl, shy and nervous, my phone sounded again.

I can meet you in Philly. There's a coffee house there. It's the 2ⁿᵈ Street Coffee Café. I began in the biz there and I hang out there upstairs. Meet you at two o'clock. The address is the name. I got the first cup.

Wow was this really happening, I decided to take control of my life for once and go after the stories I wanted to write and now I was going to possibly have my foot in the door per se. I replied:

Sounds great…I'll be there

Of course I would be there. That is all that I could say to him without sounding too over anxious. I smiled to myself and opened my car and positioned myself behind the wheel ready to start to take control of my life.

I drove out of the city skyline to my townhouse. I had just begun to make it my new home over the past few months. The collapse of my marriage was devastating. My husband of ten years, Thomas, came to an epiphany that he just wasn't in love with me anymore. He had taken me to bed and poured his heart out about how we were soul mates and destined to be together in the end, but there was something missing for him. As we made love that evening trying, I thought, to save or recapture what he felt he was lacking, I was unaware that this was his goodbye to me. He held me in his arms until dawn, but when I awoke he had left and moved out. I broke down and since I was always the one in the shadows of him, I had no real confidence to stand alone or walk tall. I was lost and lacked all confidence in my ability to love another. I didn't find out right away, but the dark, ugly truth eventually made it out into the open. The fact was that Thomas found someone else, but apparently did not want to come right out and tell me that himself.

We met in college, as I was deciding to be an English Major to write or do something like that with my degree; he had all his ducks in a row and set goals and was heading for the big business world. He had followed in his family's steps and was soon interning with a leading financial company and heading for the top. Great pay, high-rise condo in the city, convertible automobile of the latest year and me as his wing person, just along for the ride and always in the shadows. He loved me I know but I always felt he could do better with someone showier, someone that wanted the life that he sought after. For me hanging in sweatpants and cami tops all day and writing different poems and stories was pure satisfaction. We had been in love and enjoyed so many memories together for ten years. He kept striving for the top so we put off any plans of starting a family and I was content with that as I had come from a slightly dysfunctional family that the peace and calm of just him and I was perfect.

We had a beautiful over the top wedding with all the trimmings. Thomas's family planned it all and the only say I got was that I loved crème tea roses with dark pink edges and so on my wedding day the only thing I remember smiling at was that there were a few of my favorite flowers. I really just wanted it simple but he wanted to show the world that he was getting married, only for me to find out later that the company he was working for wanted their employees married to show a secure status and responsibility. Now I wonder if he was really in love with me or was it a business tactic.

Pulling into my driveway, I was finally reaching a comfort level in my life that took so long to get to after my breakdown. My townhome was quite comfortable with several extra rooms. One of the rooms held my desk and all my writings strewn about and another was filled with music for me to enjoy as I wrote. It also contained various art pieces, treasures I carefully selected. These rooms became a source of comfort for me, it became my tiny slice of heaven, a safety net for me to be in and feel secure.

I threw my keys on the table in the entranceway and entered my bedroom and saw all the clothing choices I picked through earlier for the evening all over the floor. I laughed at my mess and climbed up onto my bed. I reached for my notebook, tucked my knees comfortably and began to write a handwritten note for Max Rand.

Max Rand:

As I sat this evening in the front row of your Philadelphia Concert, I was all too captivated by you. I am not certain in my lifetime that you will ever read this, my first love letter to you, nor have the opportunity to read my words as I write them. I just knew that something touched me deep inside as I sat below the stage and watched you and the band begin to perform. As the show progressed I could not take my eyes from you, not in a star struck way, but I felt I was pulled in by some force to you. I know this is crazy as I had just met you but I felt I knew you for such a long time.

My heart is not in a good place right now, I still

feel something tugging inside and I knew that you started that pull. Let me tell you that your blue eyes are so warming, they searched the crowd and landed on mine and I felt them envelope me. So many fans were on their feet tonight dancing and singing all the words to your songs. I sat firmly in my seat, mostly because I felt if I stood that my legs might weaken mainly due to how your passion was coming through in your music and it made me crumble.

Max, as I handed you my business card I wondered how I could love you and fall for you. It was almost love at first sight. I guess this is pretty sappy for me writing about you like this, and it feels as though I am gushing with my first never to be read love letter. This will be added to my Love Notes and be like my secret diary. For now I will await our next encounter and see what feeling comes to me at the sight of your face or the sound of your voice.

Maddy xo

My eyes tired from writing and I drifted into thought. I am not sure if I'm still awake daydreaming or if I have actually fallen asleep. I was again at the concert from this evening and as they announced the band, Rolling Isaac's I was looking and searching to connect with Max's eyes and there they were. He sought me out and winked and never took his deep blue eyes from me…he reached out on one song, his hand stretching toward me and almost touching me as I reached toward him. Wanting that touch, wanting that feeling…wanting a brief passing of his igniting sensation. He got on his knees and his hands were clasped around the microphone as if in prayer. He was deep in a ballad and pouring his heart into it. He looked at me and I sank, it was so very crushing, it tore at my heart.

I was all wrapped up in the sheets and woke to music coming from my programmed ring tone on my cell phone, a tune from Tenth Avenue North called *Love is Here*. I exhaled and for that moment in my dream, love was there. I was still in my clothes from the concert, twisting in the sheets. Who was calling me now, and what time was it? I glanced at the clock it was already after eight in the morning. I slept through and Jillian called. I missed meeting up with her at eight to head to the gym. I reached out and dialed her back, and told her I was so tired and slept in but would meet her later in the week.

Jillian had become my rock over the past months. She was the first to enter the door to the high rise condo my husband and I shared after he left me. She had to pick me up, carry me and take care of me for many days. She taught me to lean on myself and take control and never be so dependent on another that I would lose myself. We shared so many girl talks and girl days together. My phone now sounded with a text that she would catch me later and hoped my tiredness was because I met someone and had fun and a late night. Although she knew that had not happened over all these months and she knew that I was not seeking that she asked anyway. I had been so deeply hurt that I didn't think I could go that route ever again.

Now that I was up I stripped down and decided to take a shower and see what was ahead of me for today as I had to meet Max Rand. Just then while in thought for the afternoon my phone sounded and a text came through. I thought Jillian was reaching out again to make the gym a little later but it was from Max.

Good morning Madison, hope you're free later tonight. I have rehearsal and if our conversation goes well, you can come meet the band. It'll give them a chance to decide about you writing about us. Hope you slept well.

Wow, I stood there, completely nude, reading this and the water in the shower continued to run, if only he knew how great I slept. I dreamt of him. This was chilling to my naked body, but in such a good way.

The rest of the morning seemed to drag; it is always like this when you want to be someplace. I caught up on cleaning since my clothes were all over and also prepared an outline for my writings in hopes my project was approved.

Soon it was time for me to leave to meet him. As I was driving into the city it took me back to Thomas and me living there before. I was happy and in love then. Thomas still lived downtown, and still almost like it was written on his calendar, would call me and leave a message of how he was thinking of me each month that has passed since he left and since the divorce. Each time he would leave in the message that he knew that we would be back together sometime in the future but he needed time to find himself, or he'd say he wasn't there yet. He never admitted to me that he left me for another woman. I heard he moved on real quickly with a new office intern, that he handpicked for the position but I heard it wasn't all that wonderful lately and there was trouble early on in their new paradise. I never took his calls because as angry as I felt inside, I admit I was weak and I would have broken down and taken him back. I would have liked closure, to hear him tell me his side of what happened. After all the time that has passed, I still felt something for him for all those years together as man and wife. We all make mistakes or wrong decisions and I always believe in second chances. I think he may have been convincing and I would have crumbled.

I was going round and round on the city streets hoping to park close to the coffee shop, but luck was not on my side for parking. I finally managed to take a spot as someone was leaving but several streets over, so my afternoon arrival time was delayed by about fifteen minutes. When I arrived I walked in and was greeted by the employee behind the counter in a very friendly manner. Before I could tell him I was meeting someone he told me that Max was upstairs already. Upward I went and smiled at the idea that Max already alerted the coffee staff of my impending arrival.

Max was deep in thought and writing in a journal as I approached. He wore cool looking silver rimmed reading glasses that he had not worn on stage and a hat that snuggled down covering his ears. He looked so everyday, average, but still very breathtaking in his normalcy. I was surprised as he seemed reserved and not exposed as when he was up the stage last evening with screaming girls surrounding him. He looked simple, still drop dead good looking but he camou-flaged it this afternoon with not having a tight tee, tight jeans or the cuff bracelet. He had worn a leather cuff bracelet last evening that he had kissed before raising his hand to the crowd at the end of the show. I wanted to ask him about that gesture but figured I would in time if I saw him do it again in concert. Today, if I didn't know I was meeting him, the same Max Rand from last night, I would have passed this guy by on a street. His attire was toned down, plain loose black tee with an open buttoned shirt over top, loose and worn and torn jeans and it appeared work boots. I pulled out the chair across from him as he looked up; he was really lost in thought there for the moment.

He paused and then complimented the color of my shirt. I felt the heat as he was staring at my chest. "Madison, wow, you look so warm."

"I'm not warm, I feel fine."

"No, I mean your shirt color highlights your dark hair and sends a warm glow. I guess I am stumbling here for something nice to say. But you look good. You're good looking and you remind me of the warmer days coming." He also sniffed in the air and said, "You smell good, really good."

"I guess thank you and thank you, you may make me blush."

Wow, did he just floor me with a compliment, and he actually smelled my Light Blue fragrance, even though I only applied a trace of it. I felt shifted in my thoughts. I had to gain composure and so I blurted out nervously, "Glad you could meet me so soon." I spoke in a professional manner trying to sound more and more confident.

He smirked and simply replied "Yeah, sure absolutely." Sounding just like me last night. He asked how I liked my coffee and took the liberty of ordering some lunch selections since if this went well, he wanted me to head to meet the band so there wasn't time for food until much later.

We began talking and I explained to him that I was following my dream of writing and had certain pieces that I wanted to complete and put together in a collection. One was to get in depth with a band. Why his band? Well I had heard them play a tune months back called *Missing Ash* and during the lowest time in my life, I had downloaded it and played it too often as I wrote at home in my writing room. I dared not tell him that, all I said was, "I have heard great chatter about the Rolling Isaac's." Also, since they were a local band from Philly. I could easily attend a lot of their shows and perhaps get stories from them to write about.

I drifted in thought for a moment; here I was trying to start a conversation and hearing Thomas in my head telling me that my writings were good, although he never really cared to read them. They weren't making him the big bucks in the corporate world so he just seemed to pass me over. But I had been so in love with him, perhaps I should have ignored my passion of writing and been more in tune with him.

"Madison, hey come back"…Max was seeking my reply. I jumped as he lightly touched my hand as it lay near my untouched coffee. It felt comfortable, safe and he kept fingers on top of my hand.

"You zoned on me, where did you just go?" He asked. I apologized to him as I slid my hand out and took a sip of coffee. I told him that I drift often into thoughts that take me away for a moment but not thoughts I want to stay in.

I started the conversation explaining that if I wasn't going to be an intrusion or bother tagging along with them, I wanted to cover them and get some real raw, natural experiences of the band. The talent, their hopes, and what they gave up to have their dreams. I told him it could be for a few months or longer but that would depend on if it became bothersome for me to be with them. I knew they played in Philly often but knew they traveled about as well. I told him the travel wouldn't be a problem and would be at my own expense. In between my speaking with him I managed to take in some bites of food, but I was still nervous. I felt like I was on a first date. I was trying to settle myself and continued to tell him some of my story.

My husband Thomas made a lot of money and he thought to leave me a nice divorce settlement. He did this despite saying that we would never be over. I guess his leaving me for someone else helped him to not have the guilt of carrying on an affair and staying married. I think he felt that he could try out this new woman and if it didn't work then he would have me in the wings. I lived a simple life so the monetary agreement would surely carry me far. But I didn't tell Max any of this, I just looked into the dark blue eyes that I had dreamt of and was stunned that they were the same blue as in my dream. I told him I was in a position to do my own travel and would not be any burden to them. I did then produce for him several pieces of writing that I published in the past from being a column writer for years at the city paper and then to a few books that were out on the shelves of several bookstores. None were best sellers, but to me, humble accomplishments. I had so many confidence steps to climb in my life now but I think I was feeling like I was on the second step.

Max glanced at the portfolio of items I brought supporting my occupation and smiled. He said, "I know exactly who you are, I followed your weekly column. You wrote the editorial piece a few years ago supporting bands. It highlighted a new, up and coming band, our band the Rolling Isaac's." Max continues "I still have the clipped article someplace back on **The Wall.** That's what we call it where we rehearse and where the band tacks up our memorabilia. You should see this wall it's freaking awesome!" He flashed me a devilish smile and said. "Slapped all over are new items about us, photos of our loved ones, and many we have loved and left the next day."

I shook at that last statement; I had been drawn in by his keepsake of the article, but then stunned by the morning after thought. Thomas had left me the morning after, left me after ten years. I had been so caught up in him that I lost me.

I could feel his eyes, warmth focused in on me and I moved around in my seat. As we talked I couldn't help thinking about the other girls. I was trying to convince him to let me follow the band, but I knew I was different from them. I knew that I was about eight years older than Max

Rand. Nothing that he said or did made me feel old, but that was just one way I was different than the rest of his followers.

"What the hell, a pretty, smart lady asks to write about me and the band, I say yes, and you can start by calling me Rand. I'm done with hearing the girls scream "Max". I tune them out. You though Madison I would listen to. It also gets confusing with me being Max and my Uncle Maxwell. Rand makes it easier. So I say, it's a go," Max said.

"Then Rand it is, thank you." I cheerfully sounded, and I nodded to agree.

After a few more bites of food from Rand's lunch selections, I started to ramble a bit. I paused only when he would eat as I followed the food to the edges of his lips. I was getting easily distracted, but then I calmed myself and told Rand a little about why I was pursuing this project now. I explained that I'd been through a painful divorce and I was beginning a new chapter in my life. I offered little in the way of details, hoping to make it clear I didn't want to revisit this subject. I needed to take a moment in my life to recapture my dream and goals and was hopeful that he could help me with that. I talked innocently to him about losing love and wanting to fill my days now with work and keep busy – that love wasn't something for me anymore. Rand looked and closed his eyes for a moment and there was something else that appeared in the blue when he reopened them, something in his thoughts but I didn't press. He knew I sought out approval for this venture with them, so he again said it was no problem.

Rand said, "Madison, all of us hurt and have been cut deep. We look for a new start, if we can ever find it." I wasn't sure where that part of our conversation was heading but he smiled warmly at me.

"Ready? Let's go" he said and grabbed my hand and tucked his journal under his other arm. I felt his fingers just hold the edges of my first three fingers lightly. He never paid a tab, but left a large bill under my unfinished coffee cup. He led me down the steps, waved goodbye to the staff, and we walked out to the black Hummer parked in the very front space. He released my fingers very slowly, in a way that made me shiver. I reached in my portfolio case and pulled out my voice recorder and hit record. I began to say with excitement in my voice, "This is the start of my writing Rock Notes." He opened the door for me, as he walked to the other side, in my whisper voice that began to shake on my recorder; I added "OMG!"

We drove about forty five minutes to where they had their space to rehearse. It was out in the suburbs of the city, in Bucks County. As we pulled up onto the location I stared at the oversized, completely redone barn. It was a sight to take in. I had seen many old barns, but this has a modern twist to its exterior. The architecture was beautifully done, not where I expected a band would rehearse. There were several acres of cleared, rolling green property that surrounded it and there was a custom built home off in the corner. It was such an awesome home; it looked like something from that television show on HGTV would have built. I wondered if their rehearsals were a nuisance to the neighbors. When I questioned him on it, he simply replied that he knows the owner and the owner never complains. We had exchanged brief conversation in the car, mostly about how much mileage does the Hummer get, weather and stupid, yes stupid, conversation topics from me. I had blundered through the conversation, but most of the unspoken communication came from Rand. He often glanced over at me and smiled, just simply smiled. I put music on and when it was their music on his playlist I said stupidly, "This is a great tune." Again, Rand flashed me his simple smile, not telling me how dumb I was coming across.

When we pulled into the open area to park in front of the barn, he told me to wait. He came around and opened the Hummer door for me. Thomas had not done this in years; I always let myself out of my side. It was such a nice gesture from Rand and the start of our business together and I hoped that the band would be as comfortable and welcoming to me.

Where do I begin? The band, all too charming, and hot looking, not as charming as Rand, and definitely not the heat of Rand's looks, but they were like a band of brothers to one another. Don't get me wrong, they talked up their stories of the girls they won and tossed. Yes tossed, and their words pitted in my stomach but I knew I had to suppress that and be calm. Rand even said, "Madison, good luck with us, you may not like us, other days you may, but don't fall for any of us, we're dysfunctional."

"Who's not functional?" was shouted by one of the band members from behind us. That gave us all cause to laugh and then I then began to meet each of the band members.

Introductions began with none other than Isaac; the person the band was named after. He was a local to the Philly area, and from what I had seen one incredible guitar player. I was introduced to him as *my front row*.

I asked, "Why was I named that?"

"Rand saw you in the front row of our show and he never took his eyes off you." Isaac's answer tugged at my heart.

Isaac seemed to be the loudest of the members and oh so ready to party. He already had a few girls waiting for him. Hoping for a kiss and that he might stay with them. I'm not sure if he needed this attention as he was a confident guy. My first take on Isaac was he was the life of any party.

I was talking with him about what I do for a living, and Rand came and tugged at him for a moment. Rand said something to him and then Isaac replied, "Hell yes, to the front row chick." Just like that, I was approved to follow along with them.

The other members then came over and were introduced to me. Next I spoke with Raeford who played the drums. He was from the Midwest, Decatur, Illinois. He was the silent one of the band I was told, and he looked so much like Usher. Rand had filled me in that Raeford brought the funk and soul to some of their songs. To me, he seemed mysterious, quiet but when I saw him on the drums the evening before he went off, so I knew he had another side.

I was introduced to Ron and Kent last. Ron was their keyboard player, wearing sunglasses indoors – in the evening.

I wasn't sure what that was about but he was very friendly. Ron welcomed me aboard and told me he was from the south. He had a slight southern drawl and was very kind. Kent was from upstate in Pennsylvania, from a small town called Clarkes Summit and he was the bass player. He was the most muscular, or should I say overly muscular, he would intimidate any person at a gym. He was very solid and fit and had a shaved head and a few piercings. He said he was destined for the military until he met up with these guys and music took over. As Kent approached me, he did not hesitate to pick me up and twirl me about and then he planted, yes planted, solidly a kiss right on my lips. I was shocked for the moment and they all laughed and he released me. The only one who seemed annoyed was Rand. He shook his head "no" to Kent and then Kent smirked at him as he simmered in his joyous greeting.

Rand told the rest of the band that I was going to write about them and to be themselves and pretend I wasn't there so I could capture them raw and real as much as possible. Rand then took me over to an area that was the loft of the barn, completely furnished with sofas and chairs and a bar that overlooked their practice stage area. As he left to head down to practice he said "Madison there's beer, help yourself and get writing. I believe it will be very interesting."

I pulled out my voice recorder and spoke into it a lot of my initial thoughts. I also pulled out my portfolio and laptop and began to type and type. The title read alone on a full page – *Rock Notes*. The band practiced for several hours, I periodically got up and stretched. I turned away and decided to help myself to a beer, well a few in the timeframe and then I walked over behind the sofa area to see **The Wall** up close and personal. This was amazing; it was huge and had a backdrop on it like a brick wall. I scanned over all the contents and in the center was the band's name, Rolling Isaac's and in each area of the wall a band member had a large area of their name and keepsakes. I saw Rand's area and there were photos of him with many, many young girls. So many photos of him with his microphone, on his knees singing and it looked like he was on the verge of crying. Next to one of these photos was a beautiful photo of a girl, so model like in looks. She had dark hair similar to his in color and shoulder length like his. She also had the most beautiful blue eyes. Next to this picture, were words signed by Rand, it read, *I will forever love you Ashley.* It took my breath away for a moment and I thought that perhaps this was the love of his life. Maybe it went bad, or perhaps they were still together, although I wasn't about to ask.

I saw many newspaper clippings and articles about all of them posted all over **The Wall**. I searched to see if my column was there and it was. I reread what I had written several years ago and I was surprised at the end of the article to see a circle around my name. Yes, just below my column photo, there was a definite circle around just my name, *Freelance Columnist – Madison Tierney.*

It was a good piece of writing if I say myself and it brought the band a lot of attention. I had done research on different bands in the city and had listened to their earlier music and critiqued it and wrote a piece about their sound and their following, although I never met them. So here I was now after meeting them, and I smiled that here I was a piece of their famous **Wall**.

Throughout their rehearsal I caught many moments of Rand staring at me. He was singing and it felt as if he was driving his voice right through me. I was always a fan of Rock music and when Rand began to sing a slow ballad, I was unable to move, I felt weak as it tore me up. It was about love lost and the emptiness you undergo and time spent on love that was gone in a moment. I wasn't sure if he had glanced my way then to see the tears in my eyes but I hoped he hadn't because I didn't want him to think I was that pathetic. Love lost was definitely where I was. He glanced up to me in the loft as soon as he finished the final melody, adding another verse without anyone playing the music. It was then that I turned away with tear filled eyes and I walked over to choke down another beer hoping to dissolve the lump in my throat.

As their evening rehearsal, or should I say early morning rehearsal came to a close, he headed up to me in the loft area. Some of the band guys had earlier invited some of their friends which were girls, to come hang out near the stage during their rehearsal. I stayed up in the loft the entire time away from them putting some of my thoughts to notes. I was watching Rand as he had stopped, yet again, to kiss another pretty young girl and patted her on the ass.

When he reached me I said, "So are you spreading the love?"

He replied, "Madison, I have no love, I just make them

feel good. Actually, I feel nothing." He said, "I lost love for anything long ago." I felt bad for starting this conversation and told him I was sorry for the intrusion into his personal life. I had a few too many beers and I know I tend to get all curious and weepy when I drink. I gathered my belongings and then he pulled my hand toward him but I wasn't certain where we were going. I thought we'd go back to get my car in the city, but then he said, "Madison, come with me," in a serious, sexy tone. A few girls were hooking up with some of the band members. Isaac was loud in shouting out to two girls that they were both for him this morning. Rand never said goodbye to them, he just waved a hand up and we walked from the loft to outside into the morning darkness and then down the path toward the house just beyond.

As we walked I asked him if we were going to wake anyone at this house. I also suggested to him that I only lived out by the National Park, only about a half hour away so if it wouldn't be a problem he could just take me home instead of all the way to the city for my car. He did not answer; he simply took hold of my hand and led me closer to the grand front door. When we got in front he removed a key and opened the door to a beautiful, lavish wooden foyer. Rand then spoke. "I've had too many beers and you look beat, I say we get your car when the sun comes up." He then said as he brushed past my ear tucking a fine wisp of hair behind my ear, "Madison, make yourself comfortable in my home. You can crash down in any of the rooms upstairs. There are plenty of boxes of the band's tee shirts if you want to change, help yourself. He continued with, "You're now part of our band" and his eyes sparkled and he smiled and then he headed toward the kitchen.

"Madison what can I get you?" he asked with an intriguing tone.

While what I really preferred is to spend more time with him, even at this late hour, I replied, "I don't need anything but thank you, all I really need is some sleep." He laughed and replied, "I'm getting cases of Red Bull for you to keep up with us on the road."

"Don't worry I will keep up, today was just a long introduction."

"Madison we have only just begun, but sleep well."

It really had been a very long afternoon and evening, and I was mentally exhausted trying to process all that had happened today. I headed toward the upper level and went in the very first room to crash. I laid my body on the first bed I saw not bothering with my clothes. Since it was spring and the evening weather was nice, I had worn a crème colored lace cami top with a floral sweater over it and jeans, but I barely recall slipping the sweater over my head.

Once my eyes closed, my thoughts turned to Rand, lost soul, lost love, so similar to me but then on stage he was so confident and sure of himself and his place in the world. That confidence was something that I lacked. He attacked the stage and all his charm and stunning looks dissolved those that set their eyes or minds on him. My mind kept trailing over and over about him. His deep blue eyes, his messy dark hair that just swept over his shoulder, his towering height, his hidden inks. I could think of nothing but him.

I tensed for a moment when I felt someone hovering over me. I felt a breath and caught the scent of Rand fresh from a shower. I was lying on my side and I slightly opened my eyes. I knew I was seeing him, not dreaming. I could see him getting closer and I shut my eyes, remaining so very still. He reached down, took his curved fingers down my cheek, so slowly and tenderly and then he leaned in and kissed me on the forehead. Trailing his mouth down from my forehead he placed a soft kiss on the side of my neck and then moved upward to the tip of my shoulder and he lightly bit at my cami strap. I was so completely shocked and although I wanted to reach around and tell him I was awake, I couldn't move. I had hopes that in the darkness he didn't see me see peak out at him moments earlier. He then whispered, "Night Madison" and he tugged off my boots and pulled a light blanket over me.

When the sun appeared in the bedroom I awoke all nervous, I got up and went to the bathroom. I had to search my purse for items to make myself presentable. It had only been about four hours that I slept. I gathered my boots and put my sweater back on and went downstairs to find Rand already wide awake and in the kitchen making us some breakfast.

"I'm starving," he said looking at me like he was ready to devour me. "Madison what are you hungry for?"

He made me hesitate to answer him, I was definitely hungry for him. "I think I could eat something." My stomach was excited and jumping inside just from seeing him so relaxed and cooking.

"Your phone has been vibrating all morning."

"What's vibrating?" I was too focused on his body and didn't hear his words.

"Your phone, you left it on the steps last night with your computer."

"Oh, okay that's what was vibrating." I was still watching his body in motion, and was thinking of how I would like him to make me stir. He caught me staring at him and I looked away and then I remembered I had silenced my phone during their practice and then powered it up when we walked over to the house. I had to pull myself together so I went to retrieve my phone and I looked at all the missed messages, they were from Jillian. I hollered back, "Rand, I just need a few minutes to check my messages." I went into his main front room and dialed her back.

"Where the hell are you?" Jillian yelled. She was so worried that I hadn't called her and she stopped by my place having her own key and I was no where to be found. It took some effort to calm her but I told her briefly what had happened since the concert.

"Jillian can you take me to Philly today to get my car? I don't want to put Rand out anymore. I'll just see if he can bring me back to my house."

"I'll agree only on one condition, I want every single detail, don't leave anything out, I want all of them!" I had to put my hand over the phone as she said this. She was so loud and I hoped Rand did not hear any of this.

"Hey, I should go, I don't want to be rude, he is making

me breakfast," I whispered to her.

"No I bet you're his breakfast…but I'll come get you at noon. You can tell me then how great this sexy man is."

I didn't get to comment, as she hung up too quickly. Rand flashed me a sexy smile when I returned to the kitchen, I wasn't sure if he heard any of our conversation. I did look up at the high ceiling in his house and knew each word spoken echoed.

"Wow this smells and looks so good," I commented but wanted to say you look and smell so good.

"Madison, take notes, you can write this too, I can cook and I am very good." Again that sexy smile pursed on his lips.

Before me was a breakfast feast. There were berry filled pancakes, sliced fruit, fresh squeezed orange juice and turkey sausage links and of course coffee made just like he had ordered for me at the coffee shop and it was in a large to go cup that read 2nd Street Coffee Café. I bet he had tons of these to go cups, he said he was a regular there.

As we sat at breakfast Rand was still writing something in his journal.

"Rand, this tastes delicious, thank you."

"Madison you seem so easy to please."

"I am a simple person, but I want to know about you, can I ask you a question?"

"Ask away Madison."

"Well this is a lovely home" I began and "well did you always live here? Was it your parents'? How did you and the band meet? Who inspired your music?"

Rand began, "Hey slow down, you said a question" he paused, "and that's several questions. But, yes, this is my home; built the year after our band got our big break. I figured since my mother, Angela had passed away from cancer right before then and she left me money I would do something good. I had the recording studio built for our rehearsals. It honored her as I continued with my passion for music."

I looked at him and smiled tenderly and then wrote some notes. He continued to answer my numerous questions. "My inspiration was my grandfather Archer, he taught me music from as far back. He was great but he left this world before my mother." Rand continued, "If I ever have a son he will be called Archer after my grandfather." And there was a smile on Rand's face like a child at an amusement park for the first time. I held his look of pure love that he displayed as he mentioned his mom and grandfather, it was so endearing and then doing what I do best, I blurted out, "What about your father is he proud of you?"

"Well," Rand replied in a serious tone, "not someone I want to discuss, to me he is Paul and right now dead to me. He never really acted like a father. When my mom got ill, he couldn't handle it, he left. He hated I played music. Hated I was the singer in a band. He hated that Ashley was my biggest cheerleader. I'm young, I stayed out late, I drank and he told me I lacked responsibility and purpose. He told me to get a real job in the business world, but not be a singer in a band."

I looked at him as he answered and mouthed silently that

I was sorry. I was sorry to hear about his mother passing and his dad's desertion. I saw his eyes swell but not break, perhaps this was his love lost.

I wanted to change the subject and said, "Rand, I have lost too, most recently, my husband, Thomas. We were married ten years. He just one day up and left me, for someone at his office. The one good memory that I have from my wedding was the flowers. They were my favorite – delicate crème roses with dark pink edging. I don't want to bore you but Thomas had become my life and world for a long time. As for my family life, it's only me. I was an only child. It was lonely. I guess that is why I love Jillian so."

I never stopped. Once I got started, I kept right on going. "And, to make my life crazier, my mother, Grace left my father, John and I for my father's younger brother Jake. She and my uncle moved off to Galveston, Texas. I haven't heard from her since."

Rand responded, "Wow your mom leaving with your uncle that's hard."

"It was, and I found myself swamped with the memories of her abandoning us, of how it felt and how I knew that I'd never truly understand relationships again."

"Do you miss her?"

"I do, she is my mother, but I never knew how to reach out to her. Since I was still with my father, I didn't want to add to his sorrow of her departure. The only saving grace, per se, for my father during that awful time was that he didn't need to raise me as I was already a teenager."

"So tell me about your father."

"Well, he was a police officer; he was a little tough on me since I was his only child. He recently retired but back during his days on the beat, he was strong like a Robocop. Everyone looked up to him. His fellow officers called him Mick, but everyone else called him Mr. McCormick out of respect. He was a very strong man but her leaving us really broke him I lived it and witnessed it."

"I miss my mother and uncle being part of my life. My mother was a true romantic and very creative so I think I have her to thank for my writing traits. But the romance part I no longer have. I hope I am not boring you with my story?"

Rand looked happy that I was sharing stories with him, "Madison not at all, I like when you talk to me, you're very…interesting."

I decided to continue and told him how I met Thomas after which I took a deep breath and then let out.

"My father adores him, and when we divorced my father blamed it on me. He told me that I didn't try hard enough to love and stay with Thomas. I haven't had the chance to repair this relationship with my father, if there is any to fix. Even now my father and Thomas talk and get together, that hurts me."

"I'm sure he adores you, what's not to like." Rand took my hand into his and began to stoke his thumb over my knuckles. "Maybe in time you and your father will reconnect." Rand could see me pushing through this with pained eyes so he changed the family topic rant of mine to geography. I was immediately grateful for his attempt to distract me and got lost in Rand's story as he kept hold of my hand with his soothing light touch.

He began to tell me that he always lived in the city and loved the vibe. He also explained how his music career all began by singing at the 2nd Street Coffee Café. Later, he ran into some other musicians and it was Isaac that shouted one drunken night for them to form a band. They all agreed to pursue this venture and their dreams of making their music together. It allowed them to combine their individual musical talents. They all fell into it quite nicely and the band in turn took off from local venues to now statewide venues. They decided together to name themselves **Rolling Isaac's** as Isaac always rolled into the practice sessions late. They didn't have a demanding schedule since they tried to stay grounded in normal life, but they did have a manager to oversee their schedules and travel and bookings.

Rand told me about his Uncle Maxwell, who had been hired to be the band's manager. He was Rand's mother's brother who took a special interest in Rand after is mother died and his father left. Maxwell was very good at the finances and the other business aspects of music. Rand's Uncle Maxwell had never had any children and never married. He had built himself a nice bank account from working in the music industry early and no one to share with, except his nephew Rand. Maxwell took care of all the schedules and arrangements from the band's equipment, to venue. He kept all the big things that went into a performance with the band low key. Maxwell took care of his guys and wanted them to focus on the music. Maxwell let them do what they did well; create their tunes while he ran around behind the scenes.

Rand continued to tell me that he had been named after his uncle and always felt a strong bond with him. His uncle always encouraged Rand to write his own songs. He was very proud and never disappointed in the career path Rand chose. He believed Rand had such talent and his music was a true art form.

The knowledge of his losses pained me since I too knew that feeling of loss. Rand then started on an upbeat note to change the tempo of our conversation. "This book is going to be great! You're a good luck charm to our band when you write about us. Plus this time I'm looking forward to hanging with you." I got up to help him with the dishes and he said, "Madison, leave it, go crash in the sunroom. I know you only slept a few hours." I wasn't about to disagree. I turned to head to the other room, as we were standing very close, he brought up his hand to the side of my cheek and touched me gently. Just as he did while I lay pretending to sleep last night. I gushed inside, I could not wait to share this with Jillian, but then I stopped. If he could not love then what was this? Just to make me feel good like he had with kissing those girls last night and many other nights in the past? I was confused and so I walked out into the stunning, bright sunroom.

The décor was masculine but eclectic. Several music themed items were in there and the rays of sunshine warmed the room as I curled up in the taupe colored leather loveseat looking outdoors and taking in the property from this view.

My eyelids got heavy and I drifted.

My phone sounded and I jumped up. It was Jillian heading to my house already. Rand was lying at the other edge of the loveseat with me, leaving only about eight inches of separation between us and he was writing in his journal.

"Can I bother you? I need to get home Jillian is coming to take me to get my car. I left it parked on 5th Street yesterday."

"No bother Madison, I can take you all the way to your car."

"No, Jillian is heading to my house anyway and she lives in the city so it's not out of her way."

"Oh, that's right you have a story to tell her, she wants to hear all about us." He started to laugh.

"Oh, I guess you heard our conversation." I was blushing.

I diverted that topic and said. "I just bought a new white Audi. I just didn't want to leave it in the city too long."

"Hey don't worry I'll get you back and I'll meet Jillian." He laughed and then said, "If I don't get you to her soon your phone will never stop ringing."

Jillian was already in my driveway when we arrived. Just like so many others, she knew who Max Rand was, but she's never met him. When he jumped out and came to open my door, her eyes got large. And then, when he took my computer and belongings into his arm, she smiled brightly. When he walked up to my door and met with her, he took her hand lightly and introduced himself, and she melted. He had that way with all the girls and lately the grown women as well.

"Rand thank you so much for the ride and the writing opportunity. I will talk to you later to go over your travel schedule." I gave him a quick hug and started to move away.

He pulled me close and said, "Madison, we leave in the morning. It's going to be a packed schedule, first Florida, and then we come back to Philly for a few weeks. Then we have Atlanta, Texas and back here to Philly to regroup." He then moved one hand to touch the side of my face as his lips lingered on my cheek what seemed a very long moment. I nervously pulled my face away, and then Rand said, "I spoke with my Uncle Maxwell and all arrangements are done. We will be by around ten tomorrow morning, so you better get packing!"

He pulled me in for a hug and smiled to Jillian who was standing behind me. When he released me, I was still leaning toward him even after he had left and driven off.

Jillian whispered, voice quivering "Holy Shit!"

Excerpt from The Knot Hole

Chapter One

"I HATE THIS OLD WOOD paneling," Taryn said aloud as she poured more Liquid Gold onto the soft cloth, continuing to rub new life back into the old wood. She had been doing this job for years now. Actually, since she had been a little girl.

Some people had a favorite picture, piece of jewelry or even a special tree. Her mother had a favorite room, this sewing room, with its four wood paneled walls. It couldn't be the kind of paneling which required only a quick wipe with a damp cloth, no, for her mother it had to be real wood, the actual smell from the wood carried through the room and you felt like you just walked into a home design store.

Each year since her mother's death five years earlier, Taryn had threatened to tear out this paneling, or paint it . . . or something, but she never did. Taryn would curse and give the wooden walls stern glances. It would seem almost sacrilegious to remove it though. As a child, this wood paneling was at the center of their family. Her father had sanded and stained each panel to perfection, and then added the final coat of finish to make it as smooth and shiny as glass.

It had taken her father many evenings and weekends to complete the room making it as her mother had dreamed it should be. Her room in which she could sew, read, relax, and escape to her dreams. When her mother was in this room with the door closed, everyone respected her need to be alone. When the door was open anyone could wander in and out.

Taryn recalled these memories of her early childhood as she continued to restore the life back into the paneling. Those memories seemed to surround her in this room, and they appeared like a play in three acts. First there was the joy and love her parents shared during the timeframe that it took to complete the walls. She recalled the renovation party her mother had arranged when it was completed. It was almost as though they were welcoming a new member into the family.

The next several months had been spent in finding just the right things to go into the room. Soft shades of yellow were the dominant colors, with beautiful tan thick pile carpeting. Each frame on the walls displayed a picture or painting that held special meaning to her mother. A vision only she could "see" as she created it.

The third act occurred every summer. When school was finished for the year, her mother would bring out three cans of Liquid Gold and a bag of soft cloths she'd been accumulating for the past year. She'd hand a can and several cloths to me and to my sister, Carolyn, and we would begin a week long project of rubbing new life into mother's precious wood paneling. An annual ceremony.

It was an almost solemn experience, such was the reverence we were taught in the care of mother's wood. We worked together for several hours a day, and as we worked, my mother would tell us stories. Each one so descriptive that they gave us a visual we still carry in our minds. We knew she made up the stories and they were very good, we could hang on her words for the entire time. Each year she repeated some of our favorites from earlier years, as well as adding new ones.

As I recall some of the stories, I still find them amazing and timeless. They weren't fairy tales. They seemed real, just as though mother were telling us about a friend of hers and the experiences this friend had; conversations that had taken place. Mother loved to dream, and apparently dreamed so vividly that she was able to tell us such beautiful and seemingly real stories.

Taryn raised herself up from her knees and stretched her sore back, rubbing her tight arm muscles and rotating her head to release the kinks. Again she said aloud, "I hate this wood paneling, now that I have to do it by myself, now that there are no more stories." Taryn stood with her shoulders slumped and felt defeated by this chore. Despite this, to remove it or change it in any way would cause her mother's spirit to become restless, of this she was sure.

She could always feel her mother's love, her essence, in this room. Taryn wondered if indeed a tiny piece of her mother's soul had remained in this room to enjoy it, in peace, throughout eternity. Taryn knew she could never change the wood walls in her mother's dream room. "Well, that's enough R & R for one afternoon. Reminiscing and Rubbing!" She threw the towel into the bucket making the statement that she was done for this day.

Taryn let the water from the shower spray over her body for a long period of time. She felt the soothing sensations of the warm water refresh her from being hunched into the corner polishing the baseboards earlier. Next she quickly dressed as food was needed in her home and the weekly grocery shopping was next, along with several other stops along the way. This was always her busiest week of the year. She was determined to keep to the schedule of devoting several hours each day, in order to finish with the wood panel cleaning in one week's time.

The next afternoon Taryn was back at work, continuing to restore the shine to the walls of the sewing room. As a child she had always been amazed at the many patterns the grains in the wood contained. As she sat back in her mother's favorite chair taking a much needed break, feet propped up and drinking a glass of iced tea, she followed some of the patterns in the wood. Her hazel colored eyes came to rest on the *dream spot*. To anyone else it appeared as a flaw in the otherwise beautifully patterned wood. She remembered asking about the one dark spot on the wood, and her mother's smiling reply. With love in her eyes, she'd said she and her father had searched through many pieces of wood paneling to find the perfect circle that would be her dream spot.

It was a perfect six inch circle, darker in color than the rest of the panel. Taryn learned when she was older that it really was just a knot hole. Her mother told the story of how rough that spot had been when she'd found it, and that her father had worked sanding it by hand with very fine sandpaper to make it perfectly smooth. Once, when asked where she got all of her beautiful stories, her mother smiled that twinkle-eyed smile and told them the stories all came from her dream spot.

The first year they'd polished the wood, she noticed her mother took great care to polish the panel particularly around this area. The second year she'd told Taryn she could have the honor of polishing that panel. The third year the honor went to Carolyn. And so it went year after year, each taking a turn polishing that distinctive area. Taryn returned her attention to polishing, in order to finish the last panel for this summer's ritual cleaning. The last panel was always the one with the knot hole. Another half hour and finally it would be done.

As Taryn rubbed the familiarly scented cloth up and down with the grain of the wood, her cloth passed over the knot hole. She experienced a moment of shock as she thought it felt hot beneath the cloth. "What the hell!" she said aloud. She rubbed over the same spot again, and yes, it did feel heated. She transferred the cloth to her left hand placing her palm over the dream spot. Several things happened at the same moment. Her hand pushed easily through the knot hole, all the way to her elbow. Her body became rigid so she couldn't move.

Panic and fear immediately set in. However, she seemed unable to move, to react physically to the situation. All she could see before her was the wall and her arm from the elbow up. The rest of her lower arm and hand had disappeared into the wall . . . without a hole to disappear into! In her panic, Taryn thought this must be what it felt like to be confined in a strait jacket, fully conscious, but unable to move a muscle in her body.

"Okay, Taryn. Get a grip," she said, "breathe, in and out slowly." The fear receded a bit, as she concentrated on breathing. She'd always been the very practical member of the family. Now was the perfect time to be realistic. "Get real here, Taryn. It is impossible that what you think you see is real. Right? Right! My arm is not stuck in a wall with no hole in it."

She couldn't move her arm. Screaming for help would do no good, since no one was close enough to her home to hear her. A strangled laugh emerged from her very tight throat as she said a silent thank you that no one could see her, or she would certainly be deemed crazy. She slowly became aware of the feeling developing in her missing hand and arm. There was warmth on the skin of her hand . . . no, heat on her hand. No, her hand was *enfolded* in heat.

"Of course," she said, "my hand is outside and the sun is shining on my hand. Right, Taryn. You stuck your hand through the wall and it's dangling outside. Where is the blood?" She concentrated on her hand and the heat and felt suddenly calmed. How could she feel so calm when her . . . "Taryn" . . . a long silence followed but she was sure she had just heard her name spoken. If someone called her name then . . . "Oh, my God. Someone IS outside. They see my hand."

"Taryn." She heard it again. She seemed to recognize the voice, but couldn't identify it.

"Taryn, don't be afraid. It's only me it's your mother."

"Mother!" Taryn screeched, "Mother?"

"Yes, Taryn, it's me. Really." Her mother's voice responded. "I've been waiting for you to find the secret of my dream spot. I knew you would. Do you feel my hands on yours, Taryn?"

"I feel the heat, yes." Taryn answered.

"I'm holding your hand, Taryn."

"Mother, this isn't real. It's impossible."

"No, Taryn, it isn't real. It's a dream experience. Do you remember the stories I used to tell you when you were little?"

"Of course, Mother. I could never forget your stories."

"Those stories were my own experiences, Taryn. I knew you children would be frightened if I told you the secret of this room and the knot hole, so I never did. I knew someday you would discover the surprise on your own, in your own time. And now you have."

"Mother, my arm can't be stuck in a hole that's not there. Nor can I be talking to you. You aren't there either. I must be stressed out and don't know it. I'm hallucinating!"

"No, Taryn. You are perfectly healthy and in your right mind. It's only that your mind cannot accept what it's seeing and hearing. It's a totally foreign concept to your mind. I have been allowed to remain nearby until you discovered this, just as I knew you would. Now that you have found it, my dear child, I can continue with my own journey. Your father has been waiting for me for a long time now, so I will join him. Together, we are off to more adventures. Have a wonderful life my dear Taryn, and enjoy the dream spot. It's now yours. It will provide adventures you cannot imagine. Remember my stories, Taryn. They were my adventures. I must go now, dear. Remember always that I love you."

Taryn was stunned. She couldn't speak. She felt her muscles begin to relax and saw her arm and hand slowly emerge from the wall. She stumbled over to her mother's favorite comfortable chair and collapsed into it, totally drained and exhausted. She fell immediately into a very deep and dreamless sleep.

Taryn awakened feeling happy and refreshed. Then she remembered her experience . . . or . . . had she dreamed it while she slept? If it had really happened, it wasn't real anyway. Her mother had said it wasn't real, that it was a dream. A waking dream?

Still feeling confused, Taryn busied herself and gathered the cleaning supplies together, she quickly realized the can of Liquid Gold was on the floor in front of the last panel. The cloth was on the floor as well, just where she must have dropped it . . . if what she thought she'd experienced really had happened?

✧   ✧   ✧

TARYN SLEPT UNTIL ALMOST NOON the next day. The long nap the afternoon before had kept her awake until the early hours of the morning. In order not to think about the afternoon's experience, she read well into the middle of her latest paperback. The heroine's troubles kept her mind well occupied until sleep finally came.

She heated a cup of water in the microwave, added a tea bag and took it out to the deck to enjoy the warm summer sun. All was well with the world that spread out before her eyes, BUT, she wondered, was all well within herself, with her life, with her future? She had a good life, an easy life, a contented life. Then why am I so restless lately, she wondered. She swept back her bangs from her forehead and played lightly with her hair deep in thought.

Last night was a perfect example. She enjoyed Brandon's company and felt comfortable with him. She had been dating Brandon on occasion for about a year, but that's all it was. It was comfortable. She routinely attended fund raising events for various causes. It was always more enjoyable for her to attend with Brandon, than alone. He wasn't the great love in her life, and she knew he wouldn't be. The love that she knew would be hers someday was not there, not like the love her parents shared. She knew she wouldn't settle for less in her mate, but then, she wasn't really anxious to get married right now either. She was only twenty-four and felt she had plenty of time. He did serve a purpose aside from good company. His presence seemed to keep others from being as blatant as they might have otherwise been about their expectations of her. Taryn enjoyed a relatively easy life. She had a comfortable income, and most of her peers knew she didn't have to work for it. As a result, they had expectations that she give to each and every cause. Taryn would have done it anyway, but their attitude soured the experience for her.

She had a number of friends, but they weren't close as she and her friend Ashlee were. Ashlee had moved to the west coast when a great job offer came her way a year ago. She had met Ashlee the first day on campus as a freshman, and it was "like" at first sight. They had roomed together for the next four years. Ashlee had been her source of strength when her mother died so suddenly in her third year at State. Sadly she earlier lost her father who had died while she was still in high school. Her sister, Carolyn, had married during her senior year in college and now traveled from post to post with her career Navy husband. She had only seen Carolyn twice since her mother's funeral.

Taryn was therefore alone when she graduated from college. Ashlee accepted the invitation to come to Virginia with her, to get a job in the area and share Taryn's home. And so it had been, until Ashlee received a reply to a resume she'd sent to the west coast. It was the job she'd wanted, in order to get started in her Hollywood career as a costumer. She'd moved to California a year ago.

It was funny. Just the other day she had been rushing around with so much to do. All busy work! I really don't have anything important to do, and I'm still not sure what kind of a future I want, she thought. I don't have a burning desire for a husband or children. I'm a writer, but I don't have a fiery aspiration to write, I just do it as it comes to me. There is no strong yearning to find that grand, passionate relationship right now or if I ever will encounter that in my lifetime. Mentioning lifetime, hers had taken a very different turn on one particular day a while back.

✧   ✧   ✧

THE SUMMER AFTER GRADUATING FROM college, she and Ashlee had started out early one Sunday morning to spend the day at the shore. They'd stopped at a mini-market to fill their cooler with drinks and to buy some beach snacks. They'd also bought one lottery ticket with the change from their purchases. A few days later they found themselves with the *winning* ticket. They both already had what they considered comfortable incomes, but now they were guaranteed a very sizable check once a year, for the next twenty years. That's when Ashlee decided she could pursue her dream of living in California and began sending out resumes. Ashlee would definitely fit into the California lifestyle. She was a beautiful girl with long blonde hair and built very nice as well as already having the look of one of those female Baywatch lifeguards. Her eyes always captivated the people she met. They were a bright blue and she was often asked if she enhanced them with color contacts. Her smile too was not to be missed, it was a great asset and would be a plus to get her into the doors of the Hollywood scene.

Taryn had resigned from her job to chart a new course. She started that journey by buying out her sister's half of the house their mother had left to them to share. She had to consider that this was, at least in part, the problem. She couldn't help but wonder if it was because she didn't have to work, that the need to work was missing. During the year she'd worked as a writer for the Sun Times, she had enjoyed it. But when she no longer needed the income, it had been so easy to leave the job and take some time to decide what she wanted to do with her skills that might be a little more exciting, more rewarding somehow.

"What are you waiting for, Taryn?" She asked herself aloud. "Where is your new venture? Writing a few articles now and then? Spending long research hours at the library for the Pulitzer Prize novel you plan to write someday? Waiting for love to come and find you?" *Enough already!*

Taryn made it to Wednesday without giving into the nagging thoughts of the dream experience with her mother. She also pushed back her thoughts of what her path in life should be. She had not entered the sewing room since last Saturday afternoon. She knew she was no longer afraid of what might or might not have occurred in that room, but still she hadn't been ready to go back in and face her questions.

Taryn entered the room and walked around slowly, lightly sweeping her fingertips over the sewing machine, the love seat, the picture of a beautiful thoroughbred horse, the lamp her mother sat beside to do her delicate hand work. She stopped and turned. Slowly, she walked to the distinctive panel across the room. She thought, once again, about her hand and arm being IN the wall, of her mother's touch on her hand, and her mother's voice. Slowly, she raised her right hand and touched the knot hole delicately with her fingertips. It was cool to the touch, not hot. She hesitated a moment, then placed the palm of her hand completely over the spot. It was still cool to her touch. She waited, with her hand still on the wall. No movement. The wall remained the same.

Almost relieved that nothing had occurred, she released the breath she had been holding and turned to walk over to her mother's favorite chair. She glanced at the door as if it had spoken to her, wondering if her mother had her dreams when the door was closed and the family gave her privacy. She walked over and slowly closed the door.

She returned to the chair and sat down, tucking her legs under her body. Feeling comfortable now, Taryn wondered how her mother had used the dream spot when she'd been sitting in this chair. Feeling very foolish, but too curious not to follow her thoughts, she spoke aloud in a sarcastic tone. "Mother said you belong to me now, dream spot, and that you will show me adventures I couldn't begin to imagine. Do you have an adventure to share with me?"

Taryn kept her eyes on the knot hole, holding in her mind the memory of her mother's warm hands holding her own, as she had the other day. Taryn didn't believe that anything would occur, but the dream spot began moving slowly, as she continued to watch it and concentrate on it. It gradually increased its counter clockwise movement until it was spinning so fast it was a blur to her wide open eyes.

There was a whirring sound, like a top spinning. It was

coming across the room towards her. The faster it spun, the louder it sounded, and the closer it appeared to her. The sound seemed to slam hard into her solar plexus and she gasped for breath. It hit her like when the floor moves with a loud clap of thunder during a storm. She then began to spin, faster and faster and in a split second it stopped, she stopped, and there was total silence.

Taryn was aware she had squeezed her eyes tightly shut and now hesitated opening them. She didn't know what she might see, or if she really was being given an adventure. This is silly, this is impossible, she thought. Open your eyes, Taryn! You'll see there is no adventure, only the sewing room. Right! Okay! Here goes!

As she relaxed in order to open her eyes, she became aware of a smell. Quickly she squeezed the lids tight shut again. Smell. What do I smell? Fresh air. Sunshine. Grass. Flowers. I hear water running. I hear birds singing. I'm outside, not in my sewing room.

Slowly she opened her eyes again. Very slowly, so she could shut them quickly again if she had to. Silly, silly, Taryn. Eyes open or eyes closed, I swear you are outside, so you might as well look.

She peeked through narrow slits between her eyelids, and sure enough she was outside. Her eyes opened wide now in surprise. She was standing in a meadow filled with all kinds of wildflowers. Some she recognized, such as beautiful purple liatris, stargazer lilies, and black eyed susans'. . . others she had not seen before and therefore could not identify but their colors were all so incredibly vibrant. She could smell the light fragrances, and combined they reminded her of a bowl filled with potpourri.

She found that she was standing beside a stream. The scent was of a cool crisp rain that just passed over. The water was slowly flowing past her, lazily washing around large stones breaking the surface. The stream was very clean and clear, allowing her to see the pebbles on the very bottom.

Taryn began walking, following the direction of the water. It seemed so silent, and yet there were many sounds. The birds, the leaves rustling in the trees, the sound of the water washing around the stones. She felt very peaceful even though there were many questions hovering just out of reach of her mind. She could only feel. Calm, relaxed, peaceful. It didn't seem important, at the moment, how she had gotten here or even where "here" was.

The stream appeared to end just up ahead of where she was walking. As she got closer, she realized it was taking a sharp turn to the right. She followed around the turn and saw a wooden footbridge crossing over the water a little further ahead. The footbridge wasn't new, but it looked very sturdy. Maybe someone took special care of it as she did with her mother's wood paneling.

She walked part way across the small bridge and decided to sit down. Dangling her legs over the edge of the bridge, Taryn watched the water flow towards her and then pass beneath her. Adventure! The water was having an adventure and so was she. A career, a family, a passion for living and creating a course to follow in her life seemed very far away now, and totally unimportant.

Suddenly, she felt more than alone when she saw a movement off to her right. She turned her head and saw a man walking toward the footbridge from the opposite bank. As he came closer he raised his hand in greeting and said, "Good Afternoon." Taryn could feel him speaking to her, but it felt like he was speaking directly into her head. She knew it was crazy, but she heard him even though she was not really hearing his voice. She wondered if he was a ghost or spirit. She could see him and feel a presence but he wasn't real. She thought if she put out her had to shake his that his would pass right through hers. Taryn returned his greeting and began to stand, but he raised his hand again indicating for her to stay seated.

"May I join you for a few minutes?" He asked.

"Yes." He had nice eyes, smiling eyes, and she felt that he was a gentle man. He was tall and very lean, his skin was pale but his eyes told the story. They were gray in color and looked so deep and endless. She asked, "Are you the owner of this beautiful meadow?"

"No I'm only the caretaker or one who oversees things that occur."

"I feel like I'm trespassing. Is it okay that I'm here?" Taryn asked concerned.

"Of course, Dear. You are most welcome to be here. Are you enjoying your first adventure?"

Taryn was stunned and sure that her face registered the surprise she felt that he should know about her adventure. She asked, "How did you know why I am here?"

"Well, Dear, I've been the caretaker here for an endless amount of time, and I have dubbed this place The Passage."

"It sounds like the name of a secret place," she replied.

"Not a secret at all but for select individuals to experience." He smiled at her to put her at ease.

"I think it will be fun. Am a little nervous as you can see. Do many people come here for an adventure?" She asked.

"Oh, my, yes," he answered. "Many people have come here for their first adventure. Many people who decide to try a dream adventure have questions and doubts as to whether it's real. You might say it's a sort of the training ground for future dream adventures."

"Have you talked with many of these people?" she asked.

"Yes, that's my job. I welcome new visitors and make sure they feel comfortable. Some have expressed great anxiety over their visit here and make the choice of not having any more dream adventures."

"My mother seemed to enjoy hers long ago. She told us such wonderful stories about them. Of course I didn't find out they were real occurrences until just a few days ago. I always thought she was just a very good storyteller."

"Did you ever wonder how so many writers could write so many books and articles, and all have a different story to tell?"

Again surprise registered on her face. "You mean some authors really are writing about their adventures?" Taryn asked.

He nodded his head methodically in response to her question.

"Are you saying this place is a starting point for would-be writers?" she continued.

"Not at all. I would describe this place more as a starting point for a creative person to explore and expand their imaginative powers, no matter what their talent. However, don't limit your thoughts to that idea, for this place is far more than that."

"My mother was a very creative person in her passion for making clothing. She was a seamstress, but she only produced clothing for me, my sister and herself. And she took great care in creating her sewing room. Is that how she came to visit here?"

"Yes. In one sense. Her creativity had no boundaries. She loved to work with fabrics, textures and colors. However, she placed being a mother and wife above a career, so she never allowed her artistic ideas to reach out into the world of fashion, where, I might add, she could have been very successful. Because she was so very inventive, she extended that ability into creating a perfect room for herself. Her innovative essence was still not satisfied and that's what led her to discover the dream adventure. Many times I told your mother she should publish her stories so other people could appreciate them. She always said they were only for her children to enjoy. It was her boundaries that caused her to decide that she couldn't take a chance on becoming a known author. In her mind, that would take her away from her family and home."

"I've thought about publishing some of her stories. But mother was so against the idea, I haven't dared to do so . . .

as of yet." Taryn smiled back.

"You may do so if you like, for they are now your stories. Your mother gave them to you as she gave you the dream spot to explore if you choose to do so."

"So you know about that?" Taryn questioned.

"Yes. We keep track of our visitors and their progress."

"Somehow through that knot hole I got here, but . . . how do I get back?" Taryn questioned as she wrinkled her brow.

"Well, as soon as you have decided your dream adventure is completed you will find yourself comfortably back in your chair in the sewing room."

"Is it always that quick and easy?" Taryn voiced.

"No, Dear. Not always. Sometimes you'll find that you're not finished with your dream adventure, but that you go back anyway."

"How? Why?" Taryn was confused.

"For any number of reasons. Your body may require a meal, the phone may ring, someone may come to your door, or you may have an appointment to keep."

"You mean I can never get stuck in an adventure and not return home?"

"You, Dear, will never get stuck anywhere. You will always return home. Your mother always returned. It wouldn't be considered an adventure if you stayed in it forever. It would create a crisis in your world". He stood up. "I'll continue my walk now. Enjoy your adventures." He smiled and raised his hand in farewell. Taryn curved her lips into a soft closed lipped smile and raised her hand, offering the same gesture. Within moments Taryn heard a distant whirring sound and before she could locate its source, she was leaning back in her chair in the sewing room.

Her first thought was to wonder how long she might have been gone. She checked the light on her answering machine, but there had been no calls. She turned on the TV and flipped to The Weather Channel. It was still the same date and no more than a half hour could have passed. Funny, it seemed like hours must have passed during her adventure.

Excerpt from Derailed

Chapter One

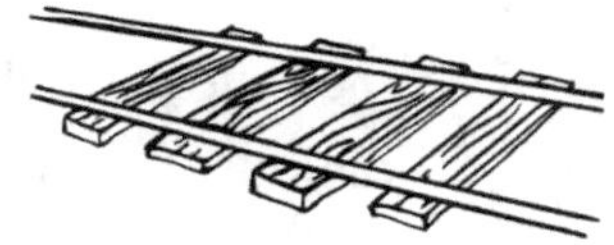

THE SUN BARELY SKIMMED THE top of the crowded metal floral basket hanging outside her door, full of blooming Abutilon (Red Bells of Summer) and crisp white Begonias, preparing to burn away the fog visiting off the ocean. Aubrey glanced out before turning the sign on the bakery door to *open*. Every morning, seven days a week, she completed the same ritual while hoping income would increase and make her dreams for *Sweet Treats* as fruitful as her pies.

Turning, she observed her business with the same contentment she'd felt looking at the sun rising over her quaint beach town. From the white wrought iron café tables with vases of fresh flowers in the center to the simple crème walls that framed the colorful, painted floral canvases, she'd created a setting designed to welcome the local residents and tourists alike. However, the bakery display cases filled with fresh baked delights and the counter top brimming with baskets loaded with fresh muffins lured them in. The scent of sliced lemons and ripe blueberries lingering probably didn't hurt, either.

Even though the revenue came from the tourist season, which was about five months of the year, most of her enjoyment occurred with the steady flow of the town locals. She had the opportunity off-season to talk with them more and engage in what was happening with the town. They stopped in often to share their stories, talk of the weather, and also mention their opinions for her love life. Most assured her she was quite attractive and her baking skills were a plus to any man's heart. Problem was she knew most of the men in the town, and many were already taken. Those not taken yet simply hadn't let their eyes cast her way.

Smoothing her floured hands on her apron, she licked her lips slowly and tasted the remnants of the red velvet frosting, today's special cupcake flavor. One more light wipe around the baskets on the counter top with her dish cloth, and she was ready to begin this new day.

Her first patrons were cheerful and friendly. Pete and Levi popped in for their morning brew, a kiss to her cheek, and sprinkled donuts; they favored the red, white, and blue, as they were police officers. As per normal, and cutting into her profits, she packaged them each a brownie and a huge chocolate chip cookie for the remainder of their shift. She never wanted to charge them as they often checked in on her, knowing she worked alone except on delivery days when a local teenager helped out.

"Aubrey, you're such a beautiful sight to see first thing in the morning," Levi complimented. She smiled. He said this to her every day he stopped in before work. Aubrey was still finishing the last of the to-go bags for them, folding the top down tightly to keep the contents fresh as Pete reached across the counter and put a twenty dollar bill in front of her. She'd learned not to dispute his actions and took it, placed it into the register, and nodded to him as her thank you.

Aubrey never thought of herself as beautiful. Her simple brown hair framed her face and landed just past her shoulders, easy for her to manage. Light makeup and a swift application of a gloss to her already pink lips and she was ready for the day with the bakery crowd.

Despite the dark brown of her eyes, a brightness always shined through. Her body was petite but well-endowed. She had to tone it down in the bakery, wearing a tee shirt with a crew neckline under her apron. She didn't need anything low cut to flaunt that her chest was a great asset.

As nice as it was to hear men tell her endearing comments, the only compliments she wanted to hear were those about her baked goods. For a moment, she played with the icing that dripped over the edge of the one pastry. Her fingertip was smoothing it out, making it perfect, yet she was remembering how she couldn't fix her recent relationship. Aubrey thought how hard it was not hearing compliments from Emerson, her ex-boyfriend she'd let go a short time back. His life and what he sought to do were too extreme for hers. He seemed to wander into doing things that were against the law. Also, as many times as she could recall, she had to keep trying to please him, and no one should have to constantly work so hard at doing that. Love should be a give and take and definitely working together.

Emerson had placed himself in the mix of some bad guys and that did not work with Aubrey at all. His one friend, Damon, gave her chills when he was around. Something about him didn't seem legit. He didn't seem like a worker on the construction site with Emerson at all. He appeared rough and had that don't mess with me attitude. He would be a fine fit as a bouncer at the local bar. Damon never said much, just observed. He trailed along side of Emerson any place he went. Thinking again of why she and Emerson parted, she licked her finger of the excess sweet, sugary icing and recalled it soured when Emerson had become too involved in drugs. She didn't want to lose her home and the bakery because of his stupidity. Cutting him loose from her life was tough but seemed the right thing to do.

The front door bells rang, and other locals came in, breaking her thoughts. The customers browsed her cases, and their eyes opened to the edible wonders she created. When she turned to assist the new customers, the officers were leaving to start their shift and sent her a friendly wave as they took bites of their breakfast. She smiled at the crumbs that left a trail behind their heavy shoes.

Aubrey went from the empty case of the pastries out front to the backroom. There she cut generous slices of her homemade pies and plated them and spent time filling the empty spaces of the ones purchased. Today she was busier than normal, but she knew that since she made enough of her treats for two days of sales that she could relax this evening. She planned to catch up with her roommate, Tessa, but for the next week, Tessa was meeting some friends in the city. She had begged Aubrey to come, but Aubrey had to run the bakery and passed on the invitation. One day, maybe, she would venture in the city for some nighttime fun. Even though Tessa seemed to want her to come along, Aubrey sensed she was just being pleasant as a roommate. It wasn't her scene in the city, and Tessa knew that. Each time she left for a few nights, Aubrey welcomed the peace and quiet of her home and a hot bath after being on her feet all day, sometimes fourteen hours.

Now Tessa, she need not work. She was the daughter of the mayor, and her father had a lot of real estate that brought in a good chunk of money. She was his only child now as he had lost his son some time ago. The town talk was that he had been shot and killed through mistaken identity. Tessa and her father rarely commented on their loss, and most didn't pry as it probably still was an open wound. The mayor, a widower who never remarried or had a current love interest, focused all his attentions on his daughter. She didn't mind that her daddy spoiled her, but she wanted some independence so she up and told her father that she was planning to move down the beach and live with Aubrey.

Despite her father's argument that the area wasn't as favorable to the eye as the homes and condos right off the streets and water's edge in the main part of town, Tessa moved in with Aubrey in the house her grandmother had left her when she passed away. The grand, Victorian style beach home with six bedrooms, five bathrooms, a wraparound porch, and a spacious second floor balcony facing the beach sounded more impressive than it looked. Mostly, the value was due to the large lot it sat on and the location. Every rainstorm, Aubrey dodged between all the rooms putting vases and buckets to catch the many leaks.

For Tessa, it gave her freedom away from her father. For Aubrey, it was the roof over her head, and the bakery and the money Tessa paid in rent kept it there. The place had a major perk, though. It was located on the beach, which had a priceless view, and Aubrey knew she wanted to keep it in her family. She was grateful that a property was hers.

Time to time, Aubrey would ask if Tessa wanted to help her out at her bakery, but it never happened. Though Tessa always fussed over herself, her makeup, her hair, and her newest, secret boy toy–never realizing a world existed beyond herself—she and Aubrey really hit it off. They both met when Tessa couldn't rid herself of a local named Wade that continuously asked her out. One day she simply told him she couldn't go out with him because she knew Aubrey had a thing for him. Begging Aubrey to go along with it, they laughed together long after the date Aubrey and Wade had was a total flop. He backed off from coming around. Occasionally, she saw him across the street, but rarely did he enter the bakery.

The afternoon slowed to a quiet one. Aubrey sat on top of the counter and swung her legs, giving them a good stretch. She kept promising to buy herself a pair of decent work shoes to relieve her aching feet, but for now, her beaten and food-spotted sneakers were all she could afford. She rested her head on the side of the commercial coffee maker, one that she shut down earlier but remained warm, and closed her eyes for what seemed to be a second.

The bells sounded on the front entrance. The noise often awoke her senses as hearing them ring alerted her to new patrons. They were nautical pieces strung together that she picked up at one of the stores in town. The long strand of shells and bells twined together gave off a delicate ring with each customer who entered.

Jumping down off the counter and straightening out her apron, she apologized to the patron before she even regarded his or her face. As she glanced up, she hesitated. A sudden awareness touched her neck, as if a strand of her hair had fallen loosely from being pinned up and swept across her skin. The feeling lingered, definitely something out of the ordinary.

"Hey, no apologies. Just wanted some coffee," the rough voice stated.

"Good morning. I am Aubrey. Your coffee is coming right up. Are you from the area?" She tried to lighten up the mood, knowing he was definitely not a local.

"No, not from here. I'm just waiting on a friend from the train station. I was feeling a bit tired so I thought the coffee would do me good." His voice was wary and reluctant.

Although he seemed polite, she watched as his eyes shifted around the place, checking it out. In that moment, she took in his large build, the few tattoos, and a definite shadow on his cheeks from not shaving. His features were chiseled, and although he appeared rough, he was handsome with a slight kindness to his face. Politeness rose from the depths of his deep voice. She was staring at him but then kept glancing away. He had that rugged sexiness that none of the locals displayed.

"Would you like cream or sugar?" Politely asking, she poured the hot coffee.

"Both," he simply stated.

"Anything else I can bring you?" She slid the coffee across the counter to him. She suggested the Red Velvet iced cupcakes, as only a few remained.

"Thank you, but no thank you," he replied in his deep voice, deliberately skimming his hand against hers when he grabbed the cup. At first it felt like their skin connected, and oddly enough, their hands remained touching for what was only a second. That brief moment, he felt an intense sensation of warmth from *her*. Tate contemplated the cupcakes because he was certain they were good, but when he eyeballed them, he caught the thick red icing. They made his stomach turn instantly.

Aubrey pulled back nervously from his intrusive touch as he took his cup of coffee. Although in that brief skin-on-skin moment, she experienced that sensation once again. He left a couple singles on the counter. When she didn't reach back out to take them from his hand, she could see disappointment in his eyes. Aubrey counted the money. She intended to tell him he'd left too much, but he was already out the door. She watched as he sat on the bench across the street and two doors down. Remembering the heaviness of his boots on his exit, she'd recognize if he came back to cause problems.

Her work day was coming to a close. Aubrey broke off a corner from a crumbled cookie that came off her tray earlier. Placing the sugary piece on her tongue, it soothed her inside. Her fingers reached up and unpinned her hair that was piled in a loose-swept pony tail. A tug on the bow around her neck released her apron, and it was scrunched and tossed into the laundry basket to take home and clean. Aubrey was heading to close up the bakery and turn the *open* sign around. As she approached the door and spun the wooden sign, the door pushed open, and he stepped in and kept her from locking up.

"Oh, please say you're not closing just yet?"

She looked at the customer and smiled pleasantly. Jackson, Tessa's cousin, was the town's best real estate agent. In fact, he had worked with her to finalize the deal on this commercial space. It needed a lot of work, but he worked a price with the lessor to fit her budget. Plus, Jackson was always helpful in the business sense. Why he had not found a lovely local to settle with was a question all the single women asked.

"No, I have a few minutes to grab you whatever you need," Aubrey courteously offered. She headed back around the front counter. Jackson scanned the displays and what pastries remained.

"I don't see any of those pecan twirls in the case. Do you have any in the back?"

"Jackson, I always have extra for you. Let me put a box together."

Aubrey went to the rear of the bakery. Boxing up the sweets for him, she started to hum. The day was over, and he was her last customer and a kind one, not like the out-of-towner from earlier that put her senses on alert.

There had been something distinctive about the stranger. She'd even thought about his facial features and how handsome he was a few times during the day. Her eyes hadn't pored over a guy that striking in a long time. She supposed he caught the train or met who he was waiting on as she hadn't seen him on the bench the last time she peered out the front window. As she placed the last gooey twirl in the box and was about to tape it shut, her hum was muffled and, in seconds, her breath taken from her.

A hand forcefully grabbed her from behind. Frantically, her arms wheeled in the air. She hit and tossed bowls filled with flour and icing, anything she could reach on the back counter. Her attacker pushed her over the butcher block, unzipping her skirt until it fell to the floor and exposed her pale thighs.

"Aubrey, I don't want to hurt you. Just don't fight me. If you fight me..." Something sharp brushed against the skin of her neck, and her eyes automatically explored where the knife that she'd cut the pies with earlier had been. Gone. Worse, she realized that no one would hear her if she did scream. The bakery was closed, and the streets outside had been deserted. And Jackson was going to rape her. "This is going to be sweet, baby girl. You might even like it." The sound of his zipper was louder than his words, a moment before he pushed her panties down.

Squeezing her eyes shut, Aubrey imagined the faint sound of bells as she prayed someone would help her. Instead, though, she felt Jackson move his hand from her mouth to her throat and then lower. She let out a light crying whimper. His hardness pressed between her legs, and she knew he was about to enter her before he hastily pulled away.

His weight lifted off her. Long moments passed as her senses returned. The sound of flesh pounding flesh filled her ears. When she opened her eyes, the stranger with the heavy boots was delivering punch after punch into precise areas of Jackson's body.

Her shaking hands pulled up her panties, and she nervously moved away from the two men. Her legs quivered, causing her to stumble as she moved toward the door. Even with her attacker lying bloodied and moaning on the floor, she could barely gather her thoughts to decide what she needed to do next.

"Are you okay?" the stranger asked. Aubrey was too frightened to answer. "I said, 'are you okay?'" She nodded, stepping back as the man approached her. Instead of taking advantage, he handed her the skirt she'd left behind, looking away for the moment to give her a bit of privacy.

Aubrey repositioned her skirt, her fingers still trembling. He waited, he opened and closed, and flexed his throbbing fists, as she smoothed the front of her skirt, apprehensively wiping her hands back and forth over the fabric several times. His movement broke her concentration on her clothing as he handed her the phone that was now covered with his bloody fingerprints and a towel. "You need to call the police and have them take this piece of trash out of here. First, though, wipe my prints off this phone. Can you do that for me?" Audrey nodded her head at his words. "Good. I'm going to leave here, but I'll wait across the street until they arrive."

He reached toward her face, his thumb set to brush her cheek. She jerked back, and he paused. When he tried again, she didn't move, and he tenderly swept his thumb across her face to erase her tears. The moist drops that formed from her eyes now coated his bloody finger.

"Aubrey, you are going to be alright." She heard her name spoken with sincerity in his voice. She was surprised he had remembered it from when she greeted him earlier in the day. Even him saying her name felt safe and reassuring coming from his mouth.

As quickly as he came in and saved her, he left. All she heard was the thump of each step of his boots until that quieted and the sound of the sirens became louder. Across the street, he remained true to his word, and as the police car promptly arrived in front of the bakery, he began his walk down past the store fronts and the few locals gathered to watch the bakery. As he crossed the street, he bent down to remove the pink icing that was embedded on the sole of his left boot from the bakery floor. He grabbed a leaf and wiped it off. Then he continued to walk far from the commotion of the street.

❖   ❖   ❖

TATE MANNING HAD JUST SAVED this beautiful girl that he knew nothing about. He had been in the right place today to prevent a brutal act. The meeting at the train station never took place; the person he was waiting on never arrived. Tate had nothing to keep him here in Cape May, New Jersey. It was a quaint town with an initial inviting sweetness about it, but his journey took him town to town. Rarely did he stay more than one night.

He saw her face as she stood near the ambulance that arrived, and he watched her shake her head to signal that she didn't want to be taken away. Again, his heart felt funny in his chest, just as it had when his fingers touched hers around his cup of coffee earlier. Tate watched, also, as they removed the scumbag that he just roughed up. He knew one more punch in the right area would have taken him out, but Tate had learned a while back to reel it in. If he didn't pull back, he'd have left a long list of dead men across the states. After all, his only mission was to travel and take down the person or individuals that were involved in his wife's murder. Too many demons played in his head because of his loss. They would never be silenced until he found closure.

Today, as much as he wanted to stay and help Aubrey with the authorities, that was not his task. He didn't want the local police department finding out that he was a cop, as that would raise a lot of flags with him just happening to be there and beating the guy near death. He wanted to walk away and continue onto the next lead in the unsolved murder that caused him to never sleep. He headed farther away from the bakery and crossed the next intersection to the bus depot. Seemed like all the traffic in this town was in front of *Sweet Treats* now. He didn't have to check for cars coming…nor would he have as he walked across the main street.

A bus pulled away just as he arrived. Tate was in no rush to head anywhere, so he bought a ticket and sat himself down to wait for the next bus. He could sit again. Hell, he had waited on the bench at the train station all day long. It wasn't too long before the bright blue and white bus rolled in. Tate stood with others to board. When the bus was filled with the passengers, it rolled out. As it left the parking lot, Tate took a quick last glimpse down the street. He was still standing at the curb, his feet reluctant to board the bus. Appeared like Tate was going to have to find a room to sleep in tonight.

He had watched the bakery the entire day, waiting on his contact, but when they never showed, he still observed *Sweet Treats* and the activity that came and went. Something kept him on the bench. A few times, he walked down the block to stretch his legs. When he came back to sit at the bench, his glance across the street caught her eyes from the bakery. Was she looking at him or for him?

He thought a few times of leaving, but decided to stick it out till late in the afternoon. He knew the bakery would be closing, and he hoped to get one last glance at her. He observed a sleek black Mercedes quickly whip into the front parking space next to her parked car. He watched her greet the man with a smile and turn the bakery sign to *closed*. Tate wasn't sure if it was her boyfriend, but he picked up on the guy seconds earlier was looking up and down the street just before she let him in. Something here was off.

Tate sensed that more than the obvious was going on. Maybe the bakery was a front, a cover-up. His days on the force pursuing drug dealers had him on high alert. His mind was stirring, and he decided to go check it out. He walked toward the front door, his head almost connecting with the red flowers that brimmed closely along the doorframe. The air was still until he detected loud banging sounds, something crashing to the floor.

There was no evidence of the guy in the front area where customers should be. He tried the door, and it was unlocked. As he approached the back, he could see the pastries scattered across the floor. He thought he heard someone cry softly. He stood and listened in the hallway. Next, all he had to hear was the words, "This is going to be sweet, baby girl. You may even like it." Fury rushed through him, pulsing blood in the veins of his powerful arms. He thought of Callie's throat cut, and he pictured this pretty woman in a situation that sounded horribly bad.

When he entered the back room, the assailant had no clue he was there. The guy had his pants down, prepared to violate her. He was focused on nothing else as his fingers deeply gripped her waist and held her painfully as her flesh reddened. He overpowered her petite, delicate frame and was seconds from taking her, entering her, and forcefully hurting her. Tate reacted. Though he wanted to kill her attacker as soon as he yanked him away from her, he paused after several hits to the man's face and chest. He knew just where to aim his vigorous pounding punches that would take him down, leaving him sprawled out motionless but still alive on the tile floor below. Tate knew the scumbag wouldn't be touching her or anyone for a long time or ever again.

Now that was messed up; he had wanted to come to this town and leave, never thinking he would be involved in something like this. Now though, he wanted to enfold her in his arms and comfort her, to stay with her. He'd known he had to leave once he helped her to dress; he knew it was best that he go. As he continued his walk to find a bed to sleep in for the evening, he rung his hands together and wiped them in his pants pockets, trying to remove the blood. He was sure he would have to sign in and register at the place he found to sleep.

9 798615 160530